ELODIE

RUTHLESS CLAWS BOOK 3

MAGGIE ALABASTER

1

JAKE

"FUCK!"

I pressed my foot down on the brake as hard as I dared. Rain fell in sheets, making the road slick. The SUV skidded for a metre or two before its tyres regained their grip on the road.

I turned the windscreen wipers up to a faster setting and focused on the lights of the car in front of me.

The lights of Ivory's much smaller Shelby Cobra. The woman liked her old, expensive toys. That might be why she liked me.

The rain reflected all the city lights, made them longer and made it harder to see.

But I saw when something huge stepped out onto the road.

I saw when she slammed on her brakes.

Her car went into a skid and hit the edge of the road.

Time stopped.

In slow motion, the small white car flipped and rolled several times. I felt every roll right into the deep of my bones. I couldn't watch. Couldn't look away.

Fuck. Elodie! Holy gods.

"Shit!" Ben's body tensed, poised like he was ready to fly right out of the passenger seat while we were still moving.

Shaking like a wet dog, I managed to steer the car to the side of the road and stopped.

I almost got tangled in the seatbelt, but managed to shove it out of the way and throw the door open.

My heart in my mouth, I bolted to the driver's side of her wrecked car. The rain fell so hard I was drenched in seconds. I barely noticed except to wipe water off my face as I crouched down beside the shattered window.

"Oh gods, Elodie." She was upside down, held in place by her seatbelt. Her face was whiter than her hair, except for the blood from a gash on her forehead. That dripped slowly onto the floor of the car. Or roof. Whatever. That didn't matter right now.

"We have to get her out of there," I said. Moving her might be dangerous, but we couldn't leave her to hang like this. We couldn't—

I sucked in a breath through wet lips. What I couldn't do right now was panic. She needed me to be calm right now. Later, when she was okay, I would freak out. Not now.

Gods, please let her be okay.

Ben crouched beside me. He nodded. As always, he was the absolute embodiment of calm. He would be just as torn up on the inside as I was, but he gave away no hint of it. I drew on that, used it to settle my pounding heart.

A groan sounded from the other side of the car.

Over my shoulder, I said to Cooper, "Go and see how Hutton is." Judging by the groan, he was still alive. I wasn't even sure I could say the same about Ivory.

I tried the door, but it wouldn't open. "We're going to have to do this through the window."

I reached inside, not giving a shit that shards of glass sliced my arms. "I'm going to hold her. When I say so, unfasten her seatbelt."

"Yep," Ben said. He wasn't a big talker at the best of times and this was certainly not the best of anything. He put his hands in place and waited. He would hold that exact position for hours and not complain. He gave new meaning to the word stoic. Good man.

I leaned in as far as I could. There was almost no room to manoeuvre in here. All I could really do was support her head and shoulders, and as much of her body as best I could.

"Okay. One, two, release." The moment Ben clicked the seatbelt free, all of her weight dropped. It felt like hardly anything at all. I kept one hand under her head to support it, while we both gripped her arms and pulled her through the window.

I sat down on the wet road and lay her across me, her neck and head on my bicep, the rest of her stretched out over my legs.

Ben shrugged out of his jacket and lay it over the top of her ruined dress.

She didn't move. She was absolutely, completely still. I couldn't even see her breathing.

Don't freak out yet, I told myself. I put my fingers to her neck to try to find a pulse.

"Come on, El," I said softly. "You have to be alive. He doesn't get to win like this." Rain mingled with tears, which slid down my cheeks and onto her face. Anyone who saw it would assume it was all rain.

Until my breath came in a ragged sob.

Ben crouched beside us and ran a hand over his head. He was drenched through, too. His white shirt clung to his upper body. He must have been as cold as I was. Truthfully, I barely felt it.

Not cold from the weather anyway. What I felt was ice cold grief.

He muttered something that sounded like, "It's my fault."

I had no idea how he figured that, but that didn't matter right now.

"Come on," I said softly. "Please don't be dead."

I closed my eyes and hung my head.

"Um, Jake?" Cooper said tentatively.

"What?" I snapped, but it was half hearted. Nothing fucking mattered anymore. Not without her.

I opened my eyes and looked down at her beautiful face.

Her eyes were open, staring at my face. She blinked.

"Oh, thank the gods." I brushed wet hair off her forehead.

"Jake," she said, her voice barely above a whisper. "It hurts—"

"Shhh," I urged. I looked up to the others.

Hutton stood beside Cooper. He appeared to be injured but more or less alive.

I would worry about him later. "We need a witch. She needs to be healed before we can move her more than we already have."

Ben scowled. "I know one who lives near here. I'll get her."

"But you hate witches," Cooper pointed out. He'd grown up since I met him. Was that only a few weeks ago? That's what this life will do to you. Poor fucking kid.

Ben looked down at Ivory, his face full of emotion. "I love her more than I hate them."

I nodded. "Take the SUV. Hutton, go with him. She can heal you on the way back. Cooper, keep an eye out for… anything."

"Got it," Cooper said. In spite of his light tone, I knew he would prefer to sit beside Ivory and hold her hand until the witch arrived. I understood, but right now we needed his vigilance. There would be time for hand holding later.

Ben trotted to the SUV and barely gave Hutton time to slip into the passenger side before he roared away.

I turned my gaze back to Ivory. She didn't look like Ivory right now, head of Ivory Claw, the biggest criminal organisation in the state. She looked like the young woman I met nine years ago. Elodie Keelan was never as naïve as she looked. Even at eighteen, she was an old soul. She went through hells and came out the other side, but not unscathed. She was a force of nature, like a deadly ice storm, in the body of a goddess. The moment I lay eyes on her, I knew our lives would be intertwined forever, one way or another.

I brushed the rain off her face. "Sorry I didn't think to bring an umbrella."

"Here." Cooper took off his jacket and handed it to me to hold over her face. It wouldn't keep the rain off much, but it was a start. "How is she?"

"She's… She's still with us," I said softly. I smiled at her. "Right? You have to stick around for a long time yet."

She moaned with what may or may not have been agreement. "Jake."

I leaned in. If this was the part where she told me she wanted to sleep, I might not be able to keep myself from freaking out. I would have to. I had to keep my shit together for her. And, to be honest, the way Cooper kept on glancing at her he was ready to lose it too.

"You should be resting," I said.

"I'm sorry," she said softly. Her eyes fluttered shut and for a moment I thought we'd lost her. She opened them again. "I shouldn't have taken off."

I smoothed more hair off her face. "Yeah, probably not. But Asshole also shouldn't have done what he did." I meant both the video and forcing his dick into her mouth. I didn't know if it went any further than that. This was certainly not the time to ask.

"Can you kill him for me?" she asked.

I chuckled. "If you want me to. But I think you would prefer to do that yourself."

She shifted position a little bit and winced in pain. I had no way of knowing what was broken inside.

"I'll help Jake kill him," Cooper said. In spite of the look I gave him, he crouched beside us and lightly kissed her forehead.

She smiled weakly. "Thanks." Her voice sounded more and more faint. "You guys are the best."

"Yeah, we are." Cooper grinned. "But you're the bestest."

"What he said," I agreed. Should I tell her to stop talking? It might be the thing that was keeping her with us. It was certainly the thing that was telling me she was still alive. She probably wouldn't listen to me if I told her to shut up anyway. She was the most stubborn, driven person I ever met. Neither of us would be where we were today if she wasn't.

"Is my car fucked?" she asked.

I looked up at it. "Yeah. I'd say so." From the look of it, the driver's side took the brunt of the crash. It must have impacted there, hard, each time it rolled over. The passenger side was slightly better off. That explained why Hutton was able to walk away.

Figures.

Ivory cared about him. She would want me to give him a break. I had given him a hard time. Still, I would have preferred she be the one to walk away.

If the witch got here soon, she still might.

I glanced over my shoulder as a car screeched to a stop beside us.

For a heart-stopping moment, I realised it could just as easily be Dagen and his goons. Cooper and I could put up a fight, but Ivory wouldn't stand a chance.

The doors opened and a ragged but otherwise healthy Hutton got out, followed by Ben and a woman who looked scared half to death. Presumably Ben hadn't given her a choice in helping us. She was a witch, she could take care of herself.

Ben all but shoved her over to Ivory and snapped, "Heal her."

"Please," Cooper said.

Ben gave him a sharp look, but didn't say anything more.

"We would appreciate it," I said. "I think she's pretty badly injured." It didn't hurt to be polite, especially since a witch could kill as easily as they heal.

She flashed me a brief smile, scowled at Ben, and knelt in the wet road and put a hand on Ivory's forehead.

Ivory twitched at the tingle of magic which I knew passed through her.

"Keep her still," the witch said.

I put a hand lightly on Ivory's chest and held her there while she twitched this way and that in obvious discomfort.

"She has a lot of broken bones," the witch said. "It's her head I'm most worried about. I'm going to heal that first. The bones probably hurt like hells, but her skull is pressing down on her brain. If I leave that, she'll die."

"Do whatever you have to do," I said. "She's tough, she'll handle it." Right now though, she didn't look very tough. She looked like a broken china doll. A fragile shard of ice.

The other three guys crouched around us, as though just by being there could help her to pull through. Judging by the way her eyes swivelled from one to the other, that was exactly what their presence would do.

Or they would all be there at the end…

I pushed that thought away. This couldn't be the end. I wouldn't let it be.

The witch bent and got to work.

Ivory started to thrash. It took all four of us to hold her still, Ben on her legs, Hutton and Cooper with an arm each and me with a hand on her chest.

She screamed out in agony. The sound tore through my ears and made them throb. It must have hurt the shit out of her throat. I would hear the sound in my dreams, but at least she was alive.

"Just a bit longer," the witch said. "I just have to relieve the pressure here… and here…"

The moment she said the last word, Ivory fell still.

The whole world went silent except for the rain falling on the road, and the engine from the few cars that whooshed by without slowing.

"Is she—" Cooper said tentatively.

"She'll live," the witch said. "I cannot guarantee there isn't permanent damage, but I got here quickly so, she should be fine."

Was she actually giving herself credit for getting

here so fast? Whatever. It didn't matter how she got here, as long as she did.

"Her bones will be an easier matter." She scooted down to around Ivory's stomach and put a hand on her arm. Whatever she did only made Ivory twitch gently, and moan, and it was over in a matter of a couple of minutes.

The witch sat back and nodded in satisfaction. "She will need to rest, but her bones are knitted nicely." She didn't even seem to notice the rain that dripped off her nose.

I realised then she wasn't much older than Ivory. She must have been scared out of her wits being dragged out into the dark in the middle of the night. Especially by a guy who wore the role of bodyguard like a second skin. If you didn't know he was a gentle giant, you might be intimidated by him. The witch obviously was. I would have to ask him later how they knew each other.

"We owe you one," I said. I meant it. Whatever she wanted, I would try to find a way to give it to her. She deserved it after this.

Even Ben gave her a grudging nod of thanks.

Cooper, being Cooper, gave her a hug. She gave him an uncomfortable hug back.

Hutton offered her a smile. "Thanks for healing

me too. I was gonna have a fucker of a headache otherwise."

Any other time, I would have replied to that with a sarcastic comment about him *being* a fucker, but I didn't have the energy or the heart to bother right now.

"We need to get her out of here," I said. "We'll drop you home first," I told the witch. After that, I had a plan. One that would give Ivory all the time she needed to rest, and give us all a chance to regroup. The gloves were well and truly off now. Whatever it took, we would make Dagen suffer for what he did to her. To all of us, but especially to Ivory.

When we were done, the asshole would wish he had never been born.

2

———————

IVORY

I woke with a banging headache. Where the fuck was I? My mind was fuzzy. Thinking hurt.

Gradually, I became aware of the sound of an engine and a thrum underneath me. I was covered in warm blankets, but under those I was naked.

Dagen's jet?

My eyes popped open and I started to sit up, cold terror running through my veins.

"Ivory! It's okay." Firm hands held me from sitting all the way up.

It took a good few moments to realise they were Cooper's hands. His face was only a few centimetres from mine. He lay beside me, but on top of the covers.

I glanced around and exhaled in relief before I lay back down and tried to calm my racing heart.

"It's *my* jet." The walls were off-white and smooth. Dark red curtains were drawn over the small windows. A timber door which led out to the rest of the plane, was ajar. Another door, this one leading to the bathroom, was closed.

He grinned. "Yeah. It's something else. I've never been on a plane that had a king-size bed before."

"Yes, well…" I had no response for that. "Where are we going?" And who the fuck thought it was a good idea to put me on a plane without asking me first?

He propped himself up on his elbow. "I have no idea. Jake just told us to grab a few things and get on board or get left behind."

Of course it was Jake. Who else would have done this? I would have a few words with him when I got the chance.

Cooper's expression turned serious. "You gave us all a scare back there. When we saw the car roll—"

"Yeah, I remember," I said quickly. My heart raced and sweat sprang up on my palms. I had a vague recollection of rain and a lot of pain.

And that fucking video.

Dagen and that fucking footage he texted to

everyone. When it came to being a motherfucking asshole, he got top points. He even got bonus points for that particular move. He was trying to get to me and it worked. I shouldn't have let it. I was supposed to be tougher than that.

"Jake and Ben pulled you out, but we all thought you were going to die. I mean, *they* did. I knew you would be okay." He wore emotion on his face that was so raw it made my heart hurt almost as much as my head. He was also obviously lying through his teeth. He had no idea whether or not I would be okay.

I rolled onto my side so I could look at him better. He wore a grey T-shirt that fitted his muscular body like a second skin and black track pants. "And then someone carried me onto the plane."

"Ben carried you," he said. "I don't think he trusted you with anyone else. But then Jake wanted to talk to him so I stayed back here to watch over you. Hutton is fine. He was in the car with you."

"Right." I forgot that detail. Thank the gods he was okay. I wouldn't have forgiven myself if I killed him. Unless he pissed me off and I did it on purpose. That was a whole other story.

Cooper looked like he had something to ask, but was too uncertain.

"What is it?" I asked.

"Before the crash, you seemed kinda pissed off at us. I don't mean right before, but the couple of days before that." He looked tentative, anxious.

"You want to know why I was so cold to all of you?" Was that even the right way to put it? I was trying to keep the guys at arm's length, but I still ended up fucking Jake and Hutton. Running hot and cold might be a better way to put it.

"Ben said you needed some space, but he was pretty cut up when you broke the bond with him. He loves you, you know. We all do. I tried not to be too pushy, but it's difficult. I mean, you're you."

He nodded as though that explained absolutely everything. That was Cooper. He was hot, ridiculously hot, smart and uncomplicated. He wore his heart on his sleeve and I knew he loved me with every bit of it.

Well, except for the bit reserved for his love of killing people. That was a whole other high for him.

I closed my eyes. Partly to ease the throbbing in my head and partly to compose my thoughts.

"Hutton told me Alistair Dagen thrives on two

things," I said slowly. "Power and mind fucks. He wants to own every building, every business that belongs to Ivory Claw because of the power that would bring. And along the way he's made a game of screwing with my head. I suspect he enjoys that more than anything."

I opened my eyes and looked right into Cooper's hazel ones. "He wanted to divide us. For me to be separated from the rest of you. And it worked. I was so scared of being distracted and vulnerable."

After a moment, I admitted, "I still am. But I can't do this by myself. I don't want to. I care about all of you." Okay, it went beyond caring.

"We're stronger together, if Jake and Hutton can stop fighting with each other." I grimaced.

"Yeah." Cooper grinned. "Sometimes I wonder if they're actually long lost brothers. I kinda feel like they're my brothers. Ben too. Bossy as fuck brothers, but still brothers."

It was good to know that, for the most part, everyone was okay with this arrangement. With a bit of luck, or a whole lot of ass kicking, maybe Jake and Hutton would kiss and make up.

Okay, now I was imagining them *literally* doing that. Oh my, that was a hot mental image. One that reminded me that I was definitely not dead.

"Did you watch the video?" I forced myself to

look Cooper in the face. When his expression filled with regret, I closed my eyes and turned my face away.

"Only the first little bit," he said quietly. "When I realised what it was, I turned it off and deleted it. He's a sick fuck and I'm sorry he did that to you. The four of us are going to personally make sure nothing like that ever happens again. And I'm going to rip his face off and eat it."

I nodded once. As much as I hated the thought of them seeing the footage, I couldn't hide from it.

Honestly, I shouldn't have to. Sure, the list of terrible things I did in my life was long. I've killed a lot of people and had even more killed for me. None of them were innocent and none were undeserving, but I still did it and would keep doing it.

In this case though, I was the innocent victim.

It was probably the first time since I was eight that I could actually claim innocence of any kind. But it was what it was. No one deserved to be violated the way I was.

I was a criminal, but I had some moral standards I lived up to. I refused to let underaged sex workers work in my brothel, or dance in my strip club. I refused to traffic in other people and if any of my employees violated another person, their dead body would be pulled out of the harbour the day after I found out about it. If the victim was a child, then their very badly, painfully mutilated body would be fished out of the harbour.

I was definitely not above torturing people who deserved it. Or, to be specific, letting Jake and Ben do it. Cooper too now, I guessed. They got off on that sort of thing more than I did, so I left them to it.

"So you know that…" Shit, how did I even word this? I swallowed hard.

"Some things are off limits?" he asked gently.

"At least until I'm ready," I agreed. I wanted to suck him off. It was something I got a lot of pleasure doing.

It used to be. Now, the idea gave me deeply conflicted feelings. Somewhere between wanting to do it and not even wanting to think about it ever again.

Cooper looked genuinely confused. "You know none of us would try to make you do anything you don't want, right? I mean, even if we wanted to, we wouldn't dare. You're beautiful, sexy, smart, but you're also the scariest person I know. If I did anything right now that you didn't like, you would call one of the other guys and I would get a one-way ticket to the ground."

"I would never throw someone I care about out of a plane," I said firmly. He was right about the rest of it though. If I didn't care about him and if he tried to hurt me, he would have an uncomfortable landing.

"I guess you wouldn't," he conceded. "If one of us did anything bad to you, the other three would make him suffer for much longer."

I grinned. "That's more like it."

The smile he gave me was soft and warm. He held back none of his feelings for me. Every single drop of them were written all over his face.

I didn't deserve him, not at all. He was sweet in a way I never was. He was hot enough to nail any girl he wanted, and yet for some reason he wanted me. There was still a boyish naïveté about him that I hoped he wouldn't lose. In time, he would probably end up as bitter and twisted as the rest of us.

I knew when I met him I should have given him the money for the auction, then sent him away. Giving his virginity to me was his choice, but it was also mine. I could have told him no, let him find a nice girl and live his life.

On the other hand, if his fascination for murder spilled into an otherwise ordinary life, things wouldn't end well for him. He was better off with me, killing people who were deserving.

Cooper glanced at the door that led into the rest of the plane. "You should be resting."

"Maybe I've rested enough," I said. "How long was I out?"

"A few hours at least," he said. He glanced at his watch and shrugged one shoulder. "But you almost died, so you probably need more than that."

I rolled over onto my stomach and pushed myself up onto my elbows so he could get a full view of my bare breasts. "Shouldn't I be the one to decide that?"

His eyes widened slightly. "Um. I mean, of course. But..."

"But you think one of the other guys is going to walk in and get pissed off and throw you off the plane?" I raised my eyebrows at him.

"A little bit," he admitted.

"Are you forgetting who the boss is around here?" I asked.

"Nope," he said quickly. "Are you going to pull that out every time we have an argument? Because that kind of seems like cheating to me."

I laughed softly. "I never said I play fair." I was horribly competitive. I was the first to admit that. If I had an unfair advantage, I would use it. He might have a point, though. If this was going to be a thing between me and him and me and the other guys, then maybe I needed to think of them as equals.

Or I could just keep doing what I was doing and keep them on their toes.

I leaned forward to kiss him lightly on the mouth.

"Are you sure this is a good idea?" he asked. "You almost died a few hours ago and, uh—"

He made a funny sound in the back of his throat when I threw off the covers and straddled his thighs. "Or I could just roll with it."

"Good idea." I put my mouth down onto his and kissed him, not like a woman who almost died a few hours ago, but like one who decided it was time to live my best life a whole lot better than I was doing. That included letting the guys in. Starting right now.

He wrapped his arms around me and pressed his hands lightly to my lower back. His tongue explored my mouth, while his hands ran up and down my sides.

"I almost forgot, I have something for you," he said suddenly. "It's in my pants."

I looked down at him. "Yes I can feel it." His erection was pressing into my belly.

He chuckled. "Something other than that." He

rolled us both sideways, just enough to get his hand into his pocket. He pulled out a silver chain. On the end was a pendant in the shape of a wolf's head. The black diamond from the box in his uncle's garage shone in the place of the wolf's eye.

"It's beautiful," I said softly.

He undid the clasp and hung it around my neck. "You're beautiful."

I touched the pendant lightly with my fingertips. "Thank you." I tried not to think about where the diamond came from. What mattered now was that it was something lovely from a guy I loved.

There, I admitted it to myself. That was a big step. The biggest I would take for at least the rest of the day.

I lowered my mouth back to his and kissed him until I was breathless.

That was around about when one of the other guys breezed in through the door.

"Well, that's a nice view," Hutton drawled. He ran a fingertip around the curve of my ass.

I shivered and felt myself melt even further. We had barely done anything and I was ready to turn into a puddle. I was no longer in a position to judge anyone for being insatiable. Somewhere along this crazy journey, the same thing happened to me. And I wasn't even mad about it.

"Care to share?" Hutton asked Cooper.

"I'm happy to," Cooper said. "As long as Ivory is."

"I'm good with that," I said and went back to kissing Cooper.

"Good." Hutton sat on the end of the bed and went back to tracing circles around my bare skin. They got smaller and smaller until he slid his hand between my legs and over my rear hole. He lingered there for a moment before he moved down to rub his fingers over my clit and pussy.

I drew up my knees to open myself out to him further.

He responded to that by slipping a couple of fingers deep into me and massaging the inside of my body.

I quivered with desire. I managed to slide Cooper's track pants down his hips to free his erection.

I gripped his hot length and worked him up and down in my hand with a corkscrew motion. I looked up at his face.

His eyes were closed with ecstasy. His cock was almost close enough for me to put my mouth around it, but I didn't. And he didn't ask me to or look as though he planned to.

I suspected he was happy to be here with me and anything else was a bonus.

Hutton worked me a little harder, then pulled his fingers out and slid them down and across my clit.

His touch and the bead of precum on Cooper's tip, drove me a little wilder. I was already as wet as hells.

I didn't realise Hutton pushed his pants down until he gripped my hips. He pulled me up until I was on my hands and knees, Cooper's thighs between them. Hutton straddled Cooper's calves and teased my pussy with his cock.

Cooper opened his eyes and his eyebrows shot up. I didn't think it was possible, but his cock got harder in my hand.

"Whoa, this is hot."

I murmured my agreement as Hutton slowly pressed his thick, pierced length into my body. The friction was immediate. Every sensation heightened a thousandfold by his ladder and this angle.

"Hot is the word," Hutton agreed. He stayed still for a while, his fingers loosely pressed against the skin of my hips.

Finally, he started to move, thrusting with even strokes that penetrated deep inside me. His piercings rubbed up and down every centimetre like ribbed fingers. Somehow firm and gentle all at once.

Cooper reached up and ran his hands around and over my breasts. He gripped my nipples lightly between his thumbs and forefingers and rolled them, then pinched them firmer. His pierced eyebrow dipped in concentration.

I kept my hand curled around his cock, pumping him slowly. When I reached his tip, I ran my thumb over the top. My hand gradually became slick with his juices.

Hutton slid out of me and guided me back down until my hips were over Cooper's cock. He pressed me down slowly, so I impaled myself on the younger wolf's eager cock.

"Gods, yes," Cooper breathed.

Hutton lay down beside us, and to my surprise he cupped Cooper's cheek and turned his face toward him.

"Hey, I dunno if you're into it…"

Holy shit, was he suggesting what I thought he was?

Apparently he was, because when Cooper moved his face toward him and their mouths met, the whole jet almost burst into flame.

Just watching them kiss made me want to come

then and there. The sound alone was… I can't even put it into words.

"Funny, I could have sworn I told them to let you rest." Jake's voice made me jump slightly, but Cooper and Hutton didn't even flinch, much less break away from each other.

I twisted around and shrugged, totally unashamed. "I'm fine."

He leaned against the door frame and crossed his arms over his chest. "Yes, you are."

I smiled sweetly. "There's room for one more." Or two, if Ben wanted to join in.

He cocked his head. "Is there? I might be a hypocrite if I stopped you from resting."

"Your cock says you'll get over it," I pointed out. The front of his pants was so tented he might break a seam.

He shook his head but took my hand when I offered it and knelt down beside me. He caught my lips with his and for a while, nothing else existed in the world but us and our mouths.

And Cooper's cock inside me.

I worked Jake's jeans open and pushed them down his hips.

In the corner of my eye, I saw Hutton and

Cooper working on each other's clothes. Shirts and track pants went flying until they were both naked.

"When in Rome," Jake said against my mouth. He broke off the kiss long enough to pull off his shirt and work his jeans the rest of the way off.

And just like that, I was surrounded by a whole planeload of smoking hot muscle and hard cocks. It's a hard fucking life, but someone has to live it. It might as well be me.

Jake brought his lips back to mine, while I gripped his cock and worked him the way I had Cooper. At the same time, I rocked my hips, riding the younger wolf while he and Hutton explored each other's mouths with their tongues.

Holy gods.

Large hands lightly rested on my shoulders. Jake's eyes flicked over behind me, but his lack of alarm told me Ben had slipped in to join us.

I broke off from Jake and twisted around far enough to press my mouth to Ben's. I would need to have a talk with him too. Breaking the bond was hard on us both, but I wanted things to be okay between us.

I kissed Ben for a minute or two, then turned back to kiss Jake again. Hutton rose to his knees and waited until we came up for air to turn my face and claim my mouth with his. He tasted like coffee and Cooper.

Cooper put his hands on my arms and pulled me down so he could kiss me as well.

I was used to being the centre of attention, but never like this. This was next level awesome and then some. I was more than the alpha she wolf, I was a goddess, and these guys were all mine.

While I leaned over Cooper, tasting his mouth and tongue, Jake opened a drawer beside the bed and pulled out a tube of lube. Silicon based, of course.

He and Ben murmured to each other and someone pressed a cool, lubed finger to my rear hole. He slipped it in and out, spreading a generous amount of lube.

When one of them pressed his cock into my ass, I had no idea which of them was. I could have turned and looked, but the idea of not knowing was strangely hot.

He waited for my muscles to relax before he pushed in deeper.

Cooper's eyes widened. "Holy shit, that feels so good."

I gave a soft moan in agreement. Two guys deep inside me was quickly becoming one of my favourite things.

The guy behind me thrust slowly and I heard Ben's groan of pleasure. So it was his cock in my ass.

That was confirmed when Jake lay down and propped himself on his elbow so his head was the same height as mine.

Hutton did the same on the other side.

I kissed Jake, long and deep and slow, then turned my head to kiss Hutton. At the same time Cooper and Ben thrust in rhythm with each other.

I felt like the centre of the universe right now, or something. Whatever it was, it felt glorious.

Jake turned my face back to him and while our tongues clashed, he slipped his hand between Cooper and I to caress my nipple.

Hutton did the same with my other breast. I heard the sound of him and Cooper kissing again. I vaguely wondered how far they would go with each other, but I knew this was a first for Cooper, so maybe not far.

Although, he was very adventurous his first time with me, so maybe…

I closed my eyes and savoured the feeling of Jake thrusting his tongue into my mouth, while the two other guys thrust into my warm body. I never wanted this to end but when I came, moaning against Jake's lips, it drew an orgasm out of Cooper.

Ben followed half a minute later. Their fast, heated strokes drove me to a second orgasm.

I came down slowly and Ben pulled out of me. He lay down on the bed beside Jake, and wiped sweat off his brow.

I slipped myself off Cooper and he and Hutton made space for me between them.

"Let me clean that up," Hutton said.

I was confused for a moment, until he moved down the bed and gently parted my knees. He bent down between my legs and slowly licked Cooper's cum away as it leaked from my pussy.

Holy gods.

He had me on the verge of a third orgasm when he moved his mouth off me and knelt between my legs. He put his cock into position and slipped into me.

At the same time, Jake knelt beside me and took his cock in his hand. "You always say I make you messy." He grinned and worked his cock back and forth, slowly at first.

Part of me wanted to take him in my mouth instead, but I almost froze at the thought. Instead, I let Cooper turn my face to him and kissed him gently.

The next thing I knew, Ben had moved over

closer and took his turn to stick his tongue almost down my throat. My lips might hurt later from all the kissing and stubble on the guys' chins.

I alternated between Ben and Cooper, while Hutton pounded my pussy.

He reached under my knees to bring up my legs to rest on either of his shoulders. With firm, even strokes, he hit me deep inside, hard enough to blissfully hurt.

With a grunt, he came, ejaculating liquid heat into my warm core.

A minute or two later, Jake came. Pearly cum squirted out of the tip of his cock and all over my breasts and belly. It was as warm as blood, but smelled like Jake, and salt, and sex. The feeling made me come one more time, hard and intense, hot inside and out. My back arched, my toes curled.

When I finally sagged back onto the bed, I was exhausted but satisfied. And surrounded by four ridiculously gorgeous, hot, incredible guys.

What more could a girl want?

3

"I WANT to know what the fuck is going on." I had a quick shower and dressed in a clean skirt and blouse. A pair of heels dangled from my fingers and my arms were crossed over my chest. "Why are we running?"

Jake looked back at me evenly. His posture matched mine and his expression was unapologetic. "We're not running."

I waved an arm around the jet. "What do you call this then?"

The guys were spread around in comfortable chairs covered in butter soft, black leather. Ben was half watching us. Cooper looked like he was asleep and Hutton was engrossed in a book. On the cover was a scantily clad blonde fairy.

I was surprised he was into that kind of thing, but I might steal it when he was finished.

"We're taking a break," Jake said. "Remember the part where you nearly died and need a rest?"

"People will think I'm running away after Asshole shared that video with everyone," I said, my voice tight.

"Since when did you give a shit what people think?" Jake asked.

"Since footage of me looking vulnerable went viral," I replied. "Did you watch it?"

He averted his eyes for a moment before he forced them back to me. "Yes. I didn't want to, but I had to know what we were dealing with. For the record, you didn't look vulnerable, just outnumbered."

"What's the difference?" I asked.

"The difference is, we will never let you be outnumbered again." He grabbed my hand and pulled me down onto his lap. I protested for a moment, but he wound his arms around me and rested his head against my shoulder.

"Not a second will go by for the rest of my life that I won't regret not being with you that night. Cooper and I, we could have killed Haigwood later. He wasn't going anywhere. We should have escorted you to your house and back again. Or sent a bunch of the other guys with you. And girls," he added quickly. "We knew Dagen was going to try something." He sighed regretfully. "I thought he would come after the business."

"He did. He burnt down Scarlett." My favourite restaurant. It was repairable, but that would take time and money. "And he made my house disappear into a sinkhole."

"I put out the order to be watching out for the witch behind that," Jake said. "She will be dealt with. So will Dagen."

"You haven't told me where we're going." I nestled down into his arms. We'd been on this plane for at least a couple of hours. As far as I could tell, I woke up shortly after we took off.

"Would you be annoyed if I told you it was a surprise?" he asked.

"Yes," I said firmly. "You know I don't like surprises." Not even the nice kind, but especially the nasty kind.

He playfully rolled his eyes at me. "Fine. We're in Victoria. I've already let the Quinn brothers know we crossed the border. They're going to come to us in a day or so."

"I would have thought Kian Quinn would want us to go to him, since this is his state," I said.

Jake shrugged. "I impressed upon him the urgency of speaking to you and explained that you were badly injured recently. Personally, I think he would welcome the chance to get out of Melbourne for a while. People seem to try to kill him a lot more often than they try to assassinate you. He'd probably welcome the chance to get away from all of that."

"I wouldn't blame him." I wondered if we could swap him and his brothers for Dagen and his pack. Let the assassins go after Dagen. The Quinn brothers and I could probably carve out some peace and quiet in New South Wales. Until our egos got in the way.

Or their cocks.

"So, we're not going to Melbourne," I reasoned. "That leaves a handful of other places where the jet can land, and we own property."

"Unless we're switching to a helicopter." He looked cagey. "Or horseback."

I snorted. "No thanks. There's only one kind of animal I want between my legs."

He placed his hands to either side of my face and kissed me lightly. "I'll keep that in mind and not suggest it as a pastime." After a moment he added,

"Does this mean you're not going to push us away anymore?" He looked adorably hopeful, but I couldn't resist playing with him. At least a little bit.

"That depends," I said slowly. "I'm still a little bit pissed off we're running away, and you won't tell me exactly where we're going."

For a moment, he looked worried I was actually pissed off at him. Then he cottoned on to my teasing.

"I should put you over my knee and spank you," he said. "I would if I didn't think you would enjoy it."

"You would if you didn't think I would have the other three guys throw you out the door," I retorted.

"That too." He grinned like the cocky bastard he was, because he knew the guys wouldn't do that to him. They were as loyal to him as they were to me. They wanted to be *like* him as much as they wanted to be *with* me. Well, except for Hutton. He was happy to be different from Jake.

That brought me to another question. "Are you and Hutton friends yet?"

Jake grimaced and glanced over at the man. Either Hutton wasn't listening or he was pretending not to pay attention to our conversation.

"I appreciate the way he stayed in contact with us while we were following you before the crash. He was texting Cooper. Those two seem to be getting along."

"Don't sidetrack," I said. "If you two are going to kill each other, I'd like to know about it in advance. So I can tell you to stop."

"I swear, I have no immediate plans to kill him," Jake said. "I don't trust him completely, but he seems to care about you."

"I care about him too," I said. "I care about all of you equally."

"But I'm your favourite, right?" Jake grinned.

"I don't have a favourite," I replied firmly. "But you and I will always have a special relationship. We've been through a lot together. Nothing will ever change that." And if he didn't like that, too bad, because that was how it was.

He gave me a sly smile. "Nothing will ever change the fact I fucked you first."

I think he expected me to roll my eyes at him, but instead I smiled softly. "No, nothing can change that. Especially given that Cooper was twelve at the time." Ben was the same age as me and Hutton was a few years older, but Cooper was definitely the pup of this little pack.

Cooper laughed. "Lucky I was too young or you would have had a fight on your hands, old man."

Jake turned to him and gave him a sarcastic smile. "I laugh because I know how much you have in your bank account, Pup. Not nearly enough to buy her virginity."

"How come you had enough?" Cooper asked. "How rich are you?"

Jake shrugged. "I stopped counting after the first billion, but that includes properties and other investments."

"If you keep getting more tattoos, you're going to end up a millionaire," I teased.

"You don't like them?" His brow furrowed.

"I love them," I said. "I just know what they cost. They're worth it though, because you look even hotter with them."

"Should I get a bunch of tattoos?" Cooper asked. He seemed genuinely curious.

"Only if you want to," I told him. "Body art is a personal thing. It's not something someone else should decide for you." Personally, I thought he was already a work of art, but the choice had to be his. I just hoped he never wanted to get any on his pretty face. I wouldn't love him any less if he did. I should tell him that, but the words wouldn't come. At some point, we would have that conversation. For now, it was nice to sit back and relax for a while.

I knew without having to ask, that Jake would have told everyone to contact me through him. I would only hear about anything work-related if he thought I needed to know it. Sometimes his over protectiveness chafed, but today I found it comforting.

The plane banked and started a slow descent towards the ground.

Hutton glanced up from his book. "Looks like we're nearly there."

"No shit," Jake said.

I gave him a sharp look.

"What? Even if we are friends, Hutton and I aren't going to stop giving each other shit. Right, Aaron?" Jake looked around me towards Hutton.

"Probably not, Jacob," Hutton agreed.

Jake grimaced. He was not a fan of his full name. He once said it didn't sound badass enough for him.

He didn't say anything now, of course. If he did, Hutton would keep calling him that until the end of time. But then, he might anyway.

I would leave them to fight it out on that one.

I leaned over to look out the window. There wasn't much to look at, just a bunch of trees. Up ahead was what looked like a small airfield. Big enough for the jet, but not big enough to be used very often.

"We're in the mountains," Cooper said. "I've never seen so many trees."

"I figured you were a city slicker," Hutton teased playfully.

"Aren't we all?" Cooper asked.

Jake chuckled. "He's got you there."

"I'm not," Ben said quietly. It was the first time I heard him speak since I woke up. "I grew up in the country. It's okay." He shrugged.

"Did you grow tomatoes and have chickens?" Cooper asked. "I mean, doesn't everyone do that in the country?"

Before Ben could answer, the jet jolted sideways.

A moment later, it dropped about a thousand feet, leaving my stomach behind.

The pilot's voice, at least as calm as Ben's, came out of the speakers in the roof of the cabin. "You've probably noticed we are experiencing some turbulence. The wind is higher than forecast. I'm going to attempt to land, but if it becomes too risky, we'll do a touch and go and bank for another try."

"Of course a drama-free break was too much to fucking ask," Jake said. He sighed out his nose in frustration.

I kissed him lightly. "Even you can't control the wind. What's the worst that can happen? It will take us a while longer to land."

"The worst that could happen is that we run out of fuel and crash," Jake said.

I cocked my head at him. "Paul is an experienced pilot. He's not going to let that happen. Besides, he's a dragon shifter. If anything bad happens, we can just jump on his back." It was one of the reasons I hired the man in the first place. He was good for defence as well as emergencies.

"He can only take three at a time," Jake pointed out.

"Well *I'll* be okay," I said, only half joking. "Maybe I should figure out now who I'm taking with me." That would be an impossible task, so hopefully it wouldn't come to that.

"Just me," Jake said lightly. "I like to stretch my legs out." He grinned at the other guys.

Without looking up from his book, Hutton flipped him off. "No one else would fit on there with your ego."

"That's true," Jake said. "There's nothing wrong with having good self-esteem. You would have it too if you were as hot as me."

Now Hutton looked up. He snorted. Without saying a word, he looked back down.

I laughed softly. "He told you," I said to Jake. "And for the record, you are all as hot as each other. Okay?"

I clung to Jake as the plane dropped again. We were buffeted so hard to the side, I almost fell off his lap.

"I think it's time for the fasten seatbelt sign." Reluctantly, I slipped off his lap and into another chair. I clicked my seatbelt into place just as the plane shuddered.

I couldn't remember when I ate last. A long time ago. That was just as well because with all this movement, I would have lost it all.

Cooper swallowed hard.

Even Ben looked a little green. I remembered he didn't like flying to begin with and this wouldn't help.

I looked out the window toward the airfield. I was no pilot, but even I could tell we were off course.

The plane banked lightly as Paul pointed the nose back towards the runway. We were almost low enough by now to skim the treetops if any were close enough.

Another gust of wind forced us to the side again.

"It's windier than the Wednesday after taco Tuesday," Jake said.

"Don't talk about food," Ben groaned.

If Hutton or Cooper had said that, Jake would probably have started to talk about hamburgers, pizza, hotdogs and whatever greasy food he could think of. Because it was Ben, he didn't say anything else. That spoke volumes about his respect for the other man. Or maybe just his lack of respect for Hutton and Cooper.

The jet approached the runway at what looked to me like an awkward angle. I wasn't sure we would even touch it, much less be able to land. Or take off again.

I have to admit that in the back of my mind I wondered if somehow Dagen did this. It was a stupid thought, because obviously wind was just a force of nature. On the other hand, so were sinkholes. If anyone would have fucked with us like that, it would be him.

I was almost certain he had done nothing. This time.

The wheels touched the dirt runway with a jarring jolt. Everything outside the windows passed by in a blur. I half expected a wheel to get stuck in a pothole and for the plane to flip, but it didn't. We reached the end of the runway and lifted off again.

Paul spoke over the speakers. "We're going around for another try. If we can't land, we're going to have to head to Melbourne." He sounded apologetic, but didn't waste time saying sorry. It wasn't as if it was his fault anyway.

The plane banked sharply to the right and came back to face the runway. The wind must have dropped a bit, because we only got buffeted a time or two more. This time, we approached the runway more or less straight.

For the first time, I noticed a couple of white SUVs parked near the airfield. Maybe they had just arrived. I glanced at Jake in question. He nodded.

"They're for us. They're even on our side."

I gave him a dark look. "Don't joke about that." I doubted Dagen would wait until we landed and take us captive again. He would just shoot us out of the sky. I hoped he would anyway. I would rather that than end up in his hands again.

I wasn't sure if the shudder that went through my body was from that thought, or the plane landing on the runway and starting to slow.

4

"IF I DIDN'T KNOW BETTER, I would think you've been planning this for a while." The sprawling house nestled in the Grampian ranges was my third favourite place to be, after Crimson and orgasmland.

Now, it was surrounded by a high fence and about a bajillion men and women dressed in Ivory Claw security uniforms. They all watched carefully as the cars approached.

The gates slid open slowly to let us through.

"I might have forgotten to mention putting up the fence." Jake shrugged. "The rest of the operation I put into motion after Dagen took you. I figured we would need somewhere to come for a break. Talking you into it was harder than I thought it would be."

"You didn't talk me into it," I reminded him. "You

had to wait until I was unconscious, and basically abducted me." I knitted my brows at him. I didn't want him to think he got off that easily.

Running away from the concert was bad enough, without seeming to be running away from Sydney.

He was unapologetic, of course. "I'll have to remember that for next time."

I socked him hard on the arm. "Whatever you're thinking, don't you dare."

"What am I thinking?" He raised an eyebrow at me in challenge.

"I don't know, but it won't be good," I said.

Cooper, who sat on the other side of Jake in the back of the SUV, said, "I won't let him do anything bad to you. Neither will Ben. Right Ben?"

"Jake wouldn't do anything that wasn't in Ivory's best interest," Ben said from the front passenger seat.

"Whose side are you on? " I asked him. He and Jake seemed happy to decide for me what was in my best interests. Cooper and Hutton too, but those two guys in particular.

"Yours," Ben said firmly. "Always. But Jake is right about needing a break. We all need one."

Sometimes I forgot Ben was also affected by Dagen taking us. He was always so stoic, so chill. It would be easy to pretend nothing ever got to him.

But the big bodyguard had feelings just like the rest of us.

Hutton too. He was almost torn apart by black wolves, then nearly killed by my driving. If anyone needed a break, it was him.

I glanced at where he sat in the very back of the SUV. He was still reading. He'd almost finished the book already. I suspected he would have preferred to be in the thick of action of some kind, but maybe this would be a chance for him and Jake to finally get along and put the past in the past. Where it fucking belonged.

As if to punctuate my thoughts, the gates slid closed behind us with a clang. The SUV followed the bend of the curved driveway and stopped in front of the house.

Before I could even touch the handle, one of the security guys hurried over to open the door for me. Another did the same on the other side.

"I feel like royalty," I muttered. "Or a movie star."

"You are royalty, El," Jake said. "You're a queen. And... Anytime you want to be a movie star, I can arrange that." He wiggled his brows.

"Don't make me sock you on the arm again," I mock growled.

"I can take it," he retorted. "Just don't knee me in the groin."

"I make no guarantees." I stepped out of the car and nodded my thanks to the security guy. What was his name? Oh, Malcolm. If I recall correctly, he was also a distant cousin. Then again, a lot of them were. White wolves tended to stick together. Not quite enough for inbreeding to be a problem, but someday it might be.

Not for me, I reminded myself sadly. Dagen took that away from me, my right to choose. Fucker.

I started up the front steps of the house, with all four guys arrayed around me. The way security snapped to attention as we walked past, I felt more and more like a celebrity. I supposed I was, in the way rich and powerful people tended to become famous for just being rich and powerful. Maybe Jake was right and I should put my hand up for my own television show. *Keeping up with the Keelans* did have a ring to it.

Who was I kidding? I was more likely to end up on an episode of *Underbelly*.

"You run a tight ship, Jacob," Hutton said appreciatively.

"Thanks Aaron," Jake said. "Or should I say Edward?"

Hutton winced. "How about you don't?"

"Edward?" Cooper looked confused.

"His real first name is Edward," Jake said helpfully. "Edward Aaron Hutton. What a mouthful."

Hutton opened his mouth, clearly intending to make some remark about his cock size. He glanced at me and closed it again. After a moment, he finally managed to say, "There's a reason I go by Hutton. Aaron is okay, but too many people think they should call me Ed."

"As in dickEd?" Jake grinned.

"This from the guy whose middle name is Lyle," Hutton retorted. "Jacob Lyle Blakesley. It suits you. Not."

"There's a reason I go by Jake," Jake said.

"Do you have an embarrassing middle name? " Cooper asked Ben and I as we stepped through the wide front doors and into the house.

"I don't have a middle name," Ben said. "It's just Benjamin Pellegrini."

"Your last name is Pellegrini?" Cooper asked. "That's so cool. The perfect name for a gangster."

Ben gave him a half smile. "Thanks, I guess."

"Believe it or not, my middle name is Bianca," I said. "My parents might have been obsessed with the colour white."

"That's pretty," Cooper said. "Pretty like you."

We all turned to him.

"What?" He looked around at us. "My middle name is John, but you probably already know that."

"Yeah, we do," I admitted. Jake probably had records on him that went back to his grades for spelling in kindergarten.

"Wow," Cooper said breathlessly.

We stepped from the foyer into the expansive, open concept kitchen, lounge and dining area. Wide windows overlooked the view down the side of the mountain. Fire crackled in a huge fireplace to one side of the room. The wall beside it held the largest sized television in existence.

The gods only knew why. Jake insisted on it. Something about watching football and movies. I didn't remember ever seeing him do either of those things. He was usually too busy torturing and killing people, and other fun things.

"If you're lucky, you'll get to see the first snows here," Ben said. "The view is even nicer then."

Nice was a typical Ben understatement. The view was spectacular on any given day. Snow made it look incredible, but so did thunderstorms and, like today, sunshine.

"Can we ski?" Cooper asked.

"Ski, snowboard, sled, roll around naked and it," Jake said. "The possibilities are endless."

"Jake means rolling around in it in wolf form," I said. Which we did do because we were Arctic wolves after all. We were made for the snow. And then sitting in front of the fireplace with a hot coffee afterwards.

We were also civilised.

The smell of something cooking wafted through the air.

"I brought the chef from Scarlett to work here," Jake said. "I figured it would be better than living on grilled cheese sandwiches."

"You think of everything," I said appreciatively. "Just a wild guess, but there's a nice hot bubble bath waiting for me upstairs?" I batted my eyelashes at him.

"Um. Yes, of course there is," he said quickly. "Just… Don't go up there for about ten minutes."

I laughed softly. He was amazing, but even Jake couldn't think of everything. Besides, if we were delayed, the water would go cold.

That would suck.

While the staff ran around running a bath and sorting out our luggage, I laced my fingers through Ben's and drew him aside gently.

"Can we talk?"

His gaze took me in for a moment. "Sure."

"Don't wander off too far," Jake said. "Remember the rules. Someone is with Ivory at all times."

"Is one of you going to watch me pee?" I raised my eyebrows at him.

"If necessary," he agreed. "Whatever it takes to keep you safe. I trust everyone here, but sooner or later Dagen is gonna try something. We'll be ready."

There was no arguing with him, even if I wanted to, so I nodded and opened the door that led out to a wide deck. It was cold out here, but the wind dropped.

Before I could say anything, Ben said, "You were right. About breaking the bond."

His words surprised me into silence.

He glanced down at the timber decking, then back up again. "When you were lying there by the side of the road, when you almost died... If I was connected to you then, I wouldn't have been able to be objective. I had to be, to go and pick up the witch. I couldn't afford to be hysterical."

I gave him a faint smile. I couldn't imagine him being anything close to hysterical, but I understood what he was trying to say.

"I'm certain you would have been as cool, calm

and collected as ever, but I wouldn't have wanted you to feel what I was feeling then." Asshole used the bond as a kind of torture device, and that's what it would have been. It could be something beautiful, but it could be something really horrible as well.

He nodded. "Exactly. I would be lying if I said I didn't miss you in my mind, but at least you're here right in front of me. You're not pushing me away."

I sighed softly. "I'm sorry for that too."

He pressed his forehead lightly to mine. "Don't be. You don't do anything without a good reason and we all understood what that reason was. Just because we didn't like it, didn't mean it wasn't totally legitimate. What happened to us, to you—" He closed his eyes. "No one can go through shit like that and just bounce back. Even you."

"You either," I said. "It was definitely not a highlight of my life. It was horrible for both of us."

"I got to spend a couple of weeks locked away with you," he said softly. "I would have preferred other circumstances, and I hate the things he did to you, but at least I was with you. There are worse things than having nothing else to do but make love to a beautiful woman."

"When you put it that way, I think I'll cancel the therapy sessions I booked for you," I said dryly.

"Don't try to pretend you weren't as scared as I was. Dagen's goons would have happily ripped you apart."

"Thinking about what they would have done to you after that would be much worse," he said. "I would happily die for you. You know that, right? Not just because it's my job."

"I know that," I said. They all would. I hoped to the gods it wouldn't come to that. I didn't want to lose any of them. I couldn't.

"So you forgive me then?" I asked.

He opened his brown eyes and looked right into mine. "There's nothing to forgive, but if there was I would always forgive you." After a moment he added, "Within reason."

"That's totally fair," I said. "I'll try not to do anything you couldn't forgive me for." I couldn't imagine what that might be, especially given who I was and the things I did on a daily basis.

"I know you will." He kissed me lightly on the mouth. "I love you."

For a moment, the all too familiar feeling of panic rose in my chest. I was both scared to say it and scared not to say it. I was terrified to feel it. No, I was terrified to *admit* I felt it. Those were three words I had never said to a guy face-to-face. But now I needed and wanted to say it four times over.

"I love you too," I said softly.

There, it was out. I said it. Now I had, I wanted to say it again and again. And I would, because I intended to live a long, long time with these guys.

"Do you think Jake got that bath ready yet?" I asked.

"Probably. Do you need someone to wash your back, or just watch your back?" He leaned his head back from mine and gave me a slight quirk of his eyebrows.

I pretended to think about that for a moment. "Why choose? Do you think you could manage to do both at the same time?"

"Not without getting a hard on," he admitted. "But I think I can manage."

"I'm sure you can." I slipped my hand back into his and we headed back inside.

"You two kissed and made up?" Hutton asked.

"I think we did that on the jet," I said. "But we had a few things we needed to say to each other. And we did that." They all knew about the situation between us, so I didn't need to explain any further. Nor did I mention that we said those three words to each other. We might all be more or less in a relationship with each other, but we didn't need to share every single detail.

"Lunch will be ready in an hour," Jake said. "Is that enough time for a bath?" The look he gave me clearly said he knew we weren't going upstairs just to wash.

For a moment I considered asking him to join us, but as much as I enjoyed threesomes and foursomes and fivesomes, I felt the need to have one-on-one time with each of the guys as well. Right now, I owed that to Ben.

I was relieved he understood about the bond, even though he was obviously clearly still hurt about it. I had considered the possibility he would ask to find another bonding stone and re-bond. Honestly, I wasn't sure what I would say if he suggested it.

Thank the gods I didn't have to make that decision. Especially given the distinct possibility the other three guys would want to do the same. I had enough shit going on in my head, without four others in there as well.

"It should be," I replied. I grabbed Jake's hand and pulled him over for a long, slow kiss. "Thank you for all of this. I know I give you hells for fussing over me, sometimes, but I like it when you do. I feel safer and I feel… Cared for."

"You are loved," he said firmly. "I love you and I

would do anything for you. I told you before, you are my universe, and I meant it."

"If I'm a universe, then you are one of my brightest stars," I told him. "All four of you are."

"I'm more of a black hole." Hutton smiled self-deprecatingly.

"Things disappear into you?" Jake asked.

"You like to suck?" Cooper asked.

"Things are irresistibly drawn towards you?" I suggested.

We all looked at Ben, who shrugged. "If the man wants to think of himself as a black hole, then who am I to argue? But I stand by what I said. You might be Jake's universe, but you're my angel."

"And my babe," Hutton said.

"And my..." Cooper frowned in thought. "Dumpling?"

I snorted.

Jake patted him on the shoulder. "Keep trying, Pup."

"But everyone loves dumplings," Cooper said. "They're tasty."

"Not as tasty as Ivory," Hutton said. "Especially with a little Cooper sauce on top." He looked smug.

Cooper's face turned pink. "I never thought I would kiss another guy. But I liked it."

"Of course you did," Hutton said. "It was me." His expression turned serious. "I've always known I was bi, but I've never felt comfortable expressing it until now. It's nice to feel accepted." He shot Jake a challenging look, as though expecting some smart ass remark from the older wolf.

For once, Jake didn't say a word. He didn't look completely convinced either, but he didn't ruin the moment.

"It makes sense that you'd feel comfortable," Cooper said. "I mean, it's me." He grinned.

"Exactly," Hutton said. "You're too adorable to resist." He punctuated that statement by kissing Cooper soundly.

"Aren't they both just too cute?" I said to Jake and Ben.

"Definitely," Ben agreed. He didn't look like he was going to kiss or touch either of them any more than Jake was, but he wasn't judging them either.

How did I get so fucking lucky? It didn't really matter how, the fact was I had and I was going to appreciate every moment of it.

"So, about that bath." I squeezed Ben's hand and we turned and headed towards the stairs leading to the upper level of the house.

"Have fun, kids," Jake said. "I'll be down here getting some work done."

I paused and turned around to look back down at him. "If there's anything you need help with—"

He waved me away. "I know you don't understand the meaning of the word 'rest,' but you're going to have to learn. That's all you'll be doing for at least the next few days." He gave me his best 'don't argue with me,' face and turned away.

"You did almost die last night," Ben said softly.

"Apparently you guys have made it your job to remind me of that every chance you get," I said, trying not to sound too bitter. I would relax for the rest of the day, but if Jake thought I'd be out of action for any longer than that, he would have to think again.

I had a black wolf to destroy.

5

"I WONDERED why anyone needed a bath this big," Ben remarked. "Now it makes sense. All five of us would fit with space to spare."

"Would you like me to invite the rest of them?" I asked teasingly.

"Hells no." He put his arms around me and tangled his fingers in my hair. "I'm happy to have you all to myself for a while." He gave me a long slow kiss, then stepped back so we could both get undressed.

He slipped into the bath first, then helped me in.

He was right, it was enormous. More like a hot tub than a bath. That was the reason I chose it, but I hadn't anticipated ever being in a position to share it with four guys. Serendipity for the win.

I slowly sank into the heavily scented water, giving my body time to adjust to the slightly too-hot bath.

"Mmm." I leaned against the side and closed my eyes. My muscles were already thanking me for taking the time to do this.

"This is nice," Ben said. He took my hand and pulled me over so my back was against his chest. He placed his hands lightly on my shoulders and started to work out the knots with slow, gentle care.

"I'm not surprised you're so tense, but we should have made you take a break a long time ago."

"It's cute that you think you could have made me have a holiday," I said.

He laughed softly. "Why have this place if you're not going to come here and unwind?"

"I bought it thinking I would do exactly that. I think knowing I could come here if I wanted to is what made me buy it."

How fucking decadent is that? To have a huge house in the mountains just for the idea of owning it. I should probably make time to come here more often.

His hands moved from my shoulders, down my arms and around to caress my wet breasts.

I leaned back against him and closed my eyes as

he palmed my nipples. I had no idea how I had any energy, much less the sex drive after the fivesome on the jet, but there it was. I was already ready for more. So was he, judging by the growing erection that pressed into the side of my hip.

His hands ghosted downward, over my belly and thighs. He slipped his hands between my legs and lightly rubbed over my clit with the side of his fingers.

I shivered and parted my legs to give him more access.

He brushed his fingers over my pussy, then turned me around to face him. He kissed me deep and long and slow. His hands cupped my ass. He lifted me up gently until I wrapped my legs around his hips.

I was already wet inside and out. His gentle touch was lovely, but I wanted him to fuck me. I positioned my entrance at the tip of his cock and pressed down, impaling myself on his rock hard, curved length.

He groaned. "You always feel so amazing."

"So do you," I said breathlessly.

He turned us around so my back was pressed against the side of the bath. "I could stay like this forever."

"Me too," I agreed. Maybe I could buy a place like

this up in the Blue Mountains and retire there. Let somebody else run Ivory Claw.

That would be heavenly, but I would get bored quickly. I would probably start up a whole new organisation, just for something to do.

Or I could spend the rest of my life with one or two of the guys' cocks inside me. That didn't sound too awful.

He locked his eyes on mine and slowly started to thrust. Lavender scented water slapped between us and threatened to go over the side and onto the floor.

The faster his strokes were, the higher the water rose.

He slipped a hand between us and rubbed my clit with firm fingers in rhythm with his cock. This wasn't going to be a quick fuck. Even as turned on as I was, my orgasm built slowly. It, like him, was taking its time.

My hands wandered all over his body, feeling his ridges and muscles and scars. He was as cut as the rest of the guys, so every centimetre of him was hard as rock. Especially all six, sorry, eight of his abs. Holy shit, he was something else. Hard on the outside, but gentle and soft on the inside. Well, soft when it counted.

"Come for me," he said eventually.

Only then I realised how ragged my breathing was. I was right on the doorstep, with my toes inside. His words made me tumble through into the blissful abyss, where nothing else mattered but his touch.

As I was coming down, he came with a series of fast, frantic strokes. Water surged to the edge of the bath with equal ferocity. As he peaked, it sloshed over the side and splashed onto the tiled floor. The sound was almost drowned out by that of his groans of pleasure.

Finally, he sagged and drew me away from the side of the bath to hold me close.

We stayed like that for the longest time, until the water started to get cold.

"We should get out, I suppose," I said reluctantly. "Before we start to look like prunes."

"Yeah, I guess so," he agreed. We unwound from each other and he helped me out of the bath. He even handed me a white, fluffy towel to wrap around myself.

"Thank you." I dried myself quickly and tucked a section of towel in between my breasts so it stayed up by itself.

I was about to leave the bathroom, when movement out the window caught my eye.

I froze. My blood ran cold.

The bathroom window had a good view out over the road and the driveway leading up to the house. And the three sleek black vehicles driving towards the front gates.

"Fuck," I whispered. Panic started to rise like a tsunami. It was Dagen, it had to be. How had he found us here so fast? How had he gotten cars organised? Questions tumbled through my brain.

"What is it?" Ben came to stand beside me, a towel wrapped around his waist. "Oh." He put his arms around me and pulled me close.

I was struggling to breathe. Was it too late to jump back in the bath and hide under the water for half an hour or so?

"It's okay," Ben said softly. "I'm not gonna let anything happen to you."

I didn't want to look out the window, but I couldn't look away.

Especially when the gates started to open.

My whole body trembled uncontrollably.

"It's okay," Ben said again. He pulled off both of our towels and held me with his warm skin directly on mine. "Jake isn't going to open the gate to Dagen."

He might not, but someone else might be

controlling them. But who would do that? Had someone betrayed us?

"Look," Ben said softly. "It's fine."

I forced myself to look. When I finally managed to take a breath, it was with relief.

Jake was trotting away from the house, towards the lead car. His body language didn't suggest he was worried. Cooper and Hutton were close behind him.

Realisation dawned on me. "Fuck. Fuck, fuck. *Fuck*. I should have anticipated he would do this."

Sure enough, when the cars stopped, Kian Quinn got out of the middle one, followed by his brothers, Tyler and Reed.

"They must have gotten into the cars the moment they got the call from Jake," I said. Thank the gods I stopped trembling by now. My mind was whirling instead.

"They thought they would catch us off guard?" Ben asked.

"That's exactly what they did," I said. I ran a hand over my hair. Thankfully it wasn't too wet, but I would have to dress quickly.

"I can go down there and tell them you're sleeping," Ben offered.

I considered the offer for a moment, but shook my head. "I want them to think we knew they were coming today. Kian obviously thought he would have an advantage over us. I want him to see he was wrong. No one takes Ivory by surprise."

Ben nodded. "Then we should both get dressed or they will definitely get a surprise."

I snorted softly. "Yes, appearing naked in front of them would absolutely send the wrong message." That begged the question though, what did I wear? If I wore one of my more revealing dresses, they might take that as an open invitation. Although, if I wore a turtleneck and a skirt down to my ankles, they would also take that as an open invitation.

Before I stepped away to the wardrobe, I squeezed Ben's hand. "Thank you. Even without the bond, you always seem to know what I need."

"That's because I spend more time watching and learning, than talking," he said. "It's a skill that comes in useful sometimes."

He was right about that. I should try it more often myself.

I released his hand and hurried to get dressed and throw on some makeup. By the time I was done, Ben was already dressed in dark jeans and a white T-shirt which accentuated his muscular physique.

I sighed dramatically. "I'm tempted to help you out of that and drag you off to bed."

He smiled. "You can do that all you want, but I'm sure you would prefer to deal with the Quinn brothers first."

"Right," I agreed. "Business before pleasure." That might as well be my motto, I'd spent so much time living by it.

"You look beautiful." He brushed his lips over my cheek. He was smart enough to know not to smudge the lipstick I just smeared over my lips.

"No, *you*." I smiled up at him.

He chuckled. "We're both beautiful. But mostly you." He took my hand and led me towards the stairs. He didn't let it go until we reached the bottom, where Jake had herded the Quinn brothers and their entourage.

Kian stood behind a dark haired woman I didn't recognise. Tyler and Reed stood a little apart, and Reed chewed on a lit cigar.

I waved my hand in front of my face. "Would you take that stinky thing outside my house?"

Reed turned to Tyler and lowered the cigar. "You heard Ivory, she wants you to go outside."

Tyler flipped him off and stepped over to me. He looked me up and down with open appreciation and smiled. "Hey, long time no see." He gave me a quick kiss on the cheek and stepped back.

Kian moved forward to do the same, but he held the woman's hand and brought her forward with him.

"Thank you for inviting us here," he said as if he wasn't two days early. "This is Blair, our girlfriend. Blair, this is Ivory."

Blair offered me a warm smile. "It's nice to meet you. The guys have all told me a lot about you."

"Don't believe a word," I said dryly. *Our girlfriend?* That would explain the vibe I got when I stepped into the room. These wolves didn't need to hunt, because they had prey of their own. From the smell of her, she was a black wolf too. She must be one hells of a woman if she could handle all three Quinn brothers. I hoped she knew exactly what she was getting into.

"Hey," Tyler protested. "We had some nice things to say."

"Ty mentioned you have great tits," Reed said. He still stood puffing on his cigar.

Kian and Blair both gave him a sharp look, but Cooper grinned.

"She does have great—" He caught the look on my face and shut his mouth with a click of his teeth.

"Please," I waved towards the couches over in front of the fire. "Get comfortable. It's so nice of you to have come so quickly." I impressed myself by managing to keep sarcasm out of my voice. Go me.

I sat down in a plush armchair and crossed my legs at my knees.

Jake perched on the arm of the chair. Hutton reclined on a couch. Cooper and Ben stayed standing, as was appropriate for bodyguards.

Our guests sat on the couches. Tyler and Reed managed to manoeuvre so Blair sat between them. Kian gave them both a dark look, but settled into the armchair opposite them.

"Jake said you've been having a bit of trouble with Alistair Dagen, and almost died last night," Kian said. "I thought it was best not to wait."

A bit of trouble? That was an understatement. The semantics didn't matter right now, I supposed.

"I appreciate your time," I said graciously. "He has been causing a bit of trouble recently. He destroyed my home and one of my businesses. He blew up one of his businesses in an attempt to get to me. And he abducted me and one of my employees."

Kian nodded. "So I've heard. He sent us some footage…"

I winced. Who hadn't the motherfucker sent that fucking video to? "Yes. I think he gets off on the idea of other people seeing that."

"That was him?" Kian asked carefully.

I swallowed. I didn't want to talk about this, but it was inevitable the moment he mentioned the footage.

"Yes it was. He also had a doctor perform surgery on me to prevent me from having children."

Blair responded to that with a sharp intake of breath. "That's awful. I can't believe—"

I turned to her. "Believe it. I didn't want to start a war with him and his pack, but he declared war on us."

"You realise what's at stake if we help you?" Kian asked.

"I know it's asking a lot," I said. "If nothing else, I would ask that you don't side with him."

My words were followed by an uncomfortable silence.

It was finally broken by Blair. "If they side with a rapist, I would kick them in the nuts."

"She really would," Tyler said. "She's an even bigger hard ass then Kian. I mean that in a nice way."

I nodded my thanks to Blair. She was easy to like. She reminded me a bit of myself, except the whole thing about being a black wolf, not a white one. Sometimes, we weren't so different.

"If we helped you," Kian said slowly. "What would you want from us?"

It was Jake who responded. "Information. Fighters if you want to send those. A spy or two. Who better to infiltrate the Onyx Ridge pack than another black wolf?"

"I could do it," Reed said. "They would never see me coming."

"You would stand out like a shark in the middle of a school of sardines," Tyler said.

"First of all, thank you for mentioning how big I am." Reed patted his groin. "But that's also the point. I stand out, and they think I'm on their side. They wouldn't need to let their guard down because they wouldn't have it up in the first place."

"You're not going in there," Kian said. "If we help Ivory, we'll do it in a way that doesn't provoke a war between the Ironhide and Onyx Ridge packs."

Reed pouted.

"I hate to say this," Tyler said, "but Kian is right. One of us going in there would provoke the shit out of this Dagen asshole. We have enough trouble already without inviting any in."

"You sounded just like Kian," Reed told him.

Tyler shrugged. "We have to grow up at some

point." He was about the same age as me. Kian was a few years older and Reed a few years younger.

"Growing up is overrated," Hutton remarked.

"I think that's the first thing you've said that I agree with," Jake told him. "It really is overrated." He turned to Kian. "We understand you can't offer personal help. The last thing we want to do is start a war that goes across state lines. We just need a little help tidying up our own backyard."

Kian sat back in his chair and ran a hand over his hair. "I could try a phone call to Alistair, to see if he'll back off, but if what you're saying he did is true, it seems unlikely he'll listen, much less comply."

I tried not to bristle at the implications that we were lying. Of course, he wasn't obligated to believe a word we'd said. The fact he was here at all said at least he was ready to listen.

"I think that might provoke him further," I said. "If he knows we spoke to you, he's going to be pissed. He will come after us hard. We need to go after him first."

Kian nodded. "I'd like to talk a bit more and then I'll consider what help the Ironhide pack can give. I'm inclined to at least offer some assistance." He looked thoughtful.

"From what I know of Alistair Dagen, he's not

going to stop at taking over your organisation. Before you took down the Onyx Ridge pack, his family was eyeing ours over the border. It's only a matter of time before he does the same. Whereas you, you've been happy to stay in your lane all these years. I would prefer to continue that arrangement."

"Me too." It was news to me the Onyx Ridge pack had looked to take over Ironhide territory, but it shouldn't surprise me. They were nothing if not ambitious. Overstepping was in their blood, along with cruelty.

"So you might say that by overthrowing the previous generation of Dagens, I did the Ironhide pack a favour," I said. I gave Kian my best sweet, innocent expression.

He wasn't fooled for a moment. I wasn't expecting him to be. I mean, I was hoping.

"You might say that," he agreed. "But that doesn't mean I have to do you one in return. Give me some time to think."

"Don't take too long," Jake said. "I can almost hear Dagen planning something from here. If we don't strike before he does, we might all be fucked."

6

"Do you think they'll help us?" Cooper asked.

I looked over to the dining table, where the four of them sat, talking in low voices.

"It's in their best interests to," I said. My phone pinged.

I raised my eyebrows at Jake. If he thought I didn't realise he stashed it in the left back pocket of his jeans, he would have to think again. He kept his phone in the right pocket, so it was obvious what it was. And yes, I was checking out his ass, that was when I noticed.

"You're not supposed to be working," he said firmly when I held out my hand.

"It might not be work," I pointed out.

"What else would it be?" He eyed my hand but made no move to pull out my phone.

"The company I hired to clear out the rubble of my house," I suggested. I wiggled my fingers at him. It was cute that he wanted to take care of me, but I was growing impatient.

"Do you want the three of us to hold him down for you?" Hutton offered.

"Fuck off," Jake told him. Reluctantly, he pulled my phone out of his pocket and tapped on the screen. He pressed his thumb on the fingerprint reader when it prompted him to.

I frowned at him. "Do I have absolutely no privacy?"

"None," he said unapologetically. "It's Freddie Whitlock. One of Harmony's boyfriends. It's work-related, isn't it?"

I leaned over to snatch my phone out of his hand. I would have to rearrange a few settings to lock him out of it. Or maybe I wouldn't bother, because he would find a way around it anyway. Asshole.

I opened Freddie's text message and read. And smiled.

"I asked him to try to access Dagen's systems. Specifically his bank accounts. It took him a while, but he got in. Money will mysteriously trickle out of

Alistair's account. Then, when the time is right, bam, it will be gone." I grinned.

Jake smiled appreciatively. "I like it. When in the hells did you get a chance to set that up?"

I shrugged one shoulder modestly. "A few hours before the charity concert." I glanced over to Hutton.

That was what I was doing before we had our conversation that led to us fucking on the couch. After that, I was too distracted to remember to mention it to anyone.

"That's fucking awesome," Cooper said. "Where is it going?"

"Some of it is going into our accounts," I said. "Several organisations who help women escape domestic violence are going to get generous donations." I didn't want his dirty money, so this way a lot of it was going to a good cause.

"I might also need to make a generous donation to the Quinn brothers," I said. I looked over to them. They didn't seem any closer to a decision.

"Wouldn't that be called a bribe?" Hutton asked.

"Of course," I said lightly. "I just thought donation sounded a bit more classy." No one would be under any illusion about what it really was, but it didn't have to sound sleazy.

"I guess you make a lot of *donations*," Hutton said.

"You would guess right," I agreed. Police, politicians, people like that. They were worth every cent to avoid a shit load of hassle. "I'm not above doing what needs to be done to get what I want."

"If we take all of his money, then do we need to attack him?" Cooper asked. "I mean, it's hard to do much of anything without the resources. Right?"

"Chances are that the moment he realises he is losing money, he'll come after us," I said. "We need to make sure our accounts are locked down tighter than a fly's asshole. He'll probably do the same when he realises what's going on. This is a distraction. Unless, of course, we manage to drain all of his accounts."

That wasn't something I could rely on. Alistair Dagen was many things, but stupid was not one of them. This would be a lot easier if he was. I could have ended this a long time ago.

"If we do that, I can buy the Maserati I've always wanted." Jake said wistfully.

"You can already do that," I pointed out.

"Yeah, but it would be much sweeter if I bought it with his money." He grinned.

I laughed softly. "I see your point. You could drive it past the park bench he's sleeping on and rev the engine really hard. That would annoy him." The mental image of Dagen being that far down on his luck was a pleasant one. I made a note to donate some of his money to homeless people. Not because I wanted him to benefit from it some day, but because they needed the help.

"I'd prefer to run him over with it," Jake said. "Several times."

"Can I come if you do that?" Cooper asked easily. "That sounds like fun."

"We could all go," Jake said. "We could make a family outing out of it. Maybe have a picnic afterwards." He grinned.

"How wholesome that sounds," Hutton said. "Do we have to wear matching outfits?"

I snorted. "No matching outfits. Jeans are fine. Hells, pants can be optional as long as Asshole is dealt with."

"Now you're talking," Jake said jokingly.

At least, I think he was joking. As far as I know, he didn't have any particular aversion to wearing pants. Although, he and the other guys seemed more than happy to get out of them around me.

"So this is our battle plan?" Ben said softly. One side of his mouth was turned up slightly. That was the only sign he too was joking. "Running over Dagen with a car?"

"Let's call that plan B," Jake said. "We have to do a lot better than that for plan A though. Something a bit more subtle. And harder for him to get away from."

"We all know what our best option is," I said softly. "We need to draw him out. The best way to do that is with the thing he wants the most. Me."

"Not a chance," Jake said immediately. "I am not going to risk you for anything."

The rest of the guys murmured and grunted their agreement.

"We have to end this," I pointed out. "This might be the easiest, quickest way to do it."

"It might also be the way you end up dead. Or worse," Hutton said. He gave me a long, measured look.

He didn't need to draw me a picture. I knew what he was talking about. Dagen would keep me alive long enough to force himself on me a time or two, then he would kill me.

"That only happens if he manages to take me." I said. "That's what you four are for. To stop that from happening. We only need me to get his attention."

"As much as I appreciate the faith in us," Jake

started, "it's too big a risk. I can't ask you to do something like that."

"You're not asking," I said. "I'm telling you this is the best way. Maybe the only way. We might catch him off guard."

I chewed my lip for a moment. I hatched an idea in my mind, but I decided not to go into details yet.

Instead I said, "If we do this right, then there's no risk to me at all." That wasn't true, there was always going to be some risk. But we could minimalise it.

"It's better than sitting around waiting for him to do something." I crossed my arms over my breasts. "I could do this without any of you."

From the expressions on all of their faces, I struck a nerve with that.

Jake even flinched. He knew it wasn't an empty threat. If they tried to stand in my way, I would do this anyway. Not without an army of white or black wolves, because I was pissed off, not stupid, but I would prefer to do this with them. I didn't trust anyone else to have my back the way they did.

Cooper raised his hand. "Is anyone else thinking we should lock Ivory in her bedroom until this is over?"

No one disagreed with that question.

"I will not be locked in an…" I couldn't resist, "an Ivory tower while you guys get on with the job."

"This is usually where she threatens to fire us all," Jake said. "But that won't fly anymore. We've all gone way past being employees." He looked directly at me. "You'll have to find some other way to threaten us. If we have to lock you away to keep you safe, that's what we'll do."

"The fuck you will," I growled. I stood and stalked a few steps away before turning and stalking back.

"Running away was bad enough. I refuse to hide." I placed my fists on my hips. "Has any one of you got a better idea than using me as bait?"

"We could fire a rocket launcher at his house," Cooper suggested.

"See?" Jake said. "That's a much better idea."

"Right," I said slowly. "Do you think the police will turn a blind eye to that? It only takes one dickhead with a phone to film it and we're screwed."

"We will happily go to prison for you," Jake said. "We would probably fight over who used the rocket launcher. That's how much we care about you."

"Rock, paper, scissors?" Cooper asked.

"None of you is using a rocket launcher," I said as they started to stretch their hands out in front of them.

Men.

The smell of testosterone was stronger than ever. Usually I liked it, but today it was almost overwhelming.

They lowered their hands. All four of them looked disappointed.

I closed my eyes and shook my head. "It's decided then. We just need to work out the details."

"Elodie—" Jake stood and put his arms around me. "If anything happens to you, I will never forgive myself."

"I'll never forgive him either," Hutton said helpfully.

Jake flipped him off.

"If you have to do this, then I'm going to be there," Ben said firmly. "In whatever capacity you need me. If this is what it takes to bring down Alistair Dagen, then I'm in."

"Me too," Cooper said. "Can we at least make the rocket launcher plan C?"

"Since we won't get down that far, you can make it plan whatever the hells you want," I told him. I almost managed to ignore when he punched the air in triumph.

I was surrounded by hot, muscular little boys. I wasn't exactly saying I wanted them to grow up, but hopefully they would show a little bit of maturity during this operation. Playing around could get them killed. Worse than that, it could get me killed. No one would forgive them for that, especially me.

Jake leaned his head on my shoulder and sighed. "Since you're going to do this with or without me, I guess I better be in as well. If I leave it to these clowns, they'll probably fuck it up somehow."

"We love you too, Jake," Cooper said. "We're a team and we couldn't do it without you. We need your badass skills."

"You'll need mine too," Hutton said. He looked less than thrilled with the idea of going after Dagen like this, but he was as determined as I was to put a stop to all of this. "I don't suppose—" He shifted in his seat. "We could use me as bait instead. He wants me dead as much as he wants you dead."

"Now there's an idea I could get behind," Jake said.

Hutton shot him a look and rolled his eyes. "He wants you too."

"I will happily take Elodie's place," Jake said easily.

"He would have both of you killed before you got anywhere near him," I pointed out. "He wants to toy with me. That gives us time."

My stomach turned violently at the idea. I had to shove down the starting edge of a panic attack. If we did this right, the guys would be there before the whole thing went sideways. If we messed it up, I would have to live with the consequences of that. Assuming I got to live at all. If I didn't, then Jake and my sister might have to finish what I started.

"I hate to say it, but she's right," Hutton said.

Ben nodded his agreement. "He only kept me alive to screw with Ivory. I doubt he will make the same mistake again."

"He kept me alive because the idea of a white wolf working for him amused him," Hutton said. "And so he could test my loyalty to him. Which I failed, as you know. My loyalty is with Ivory. He knows that for certain now. He's definitely not going to let me near his organisation again."

"No, he's not," I agreed. "He would prefer to work with witches than other wolves." I wrinkled my nose.

"Most of the wolves don't want to work with him anyway," Ben said. "Otherwise why would he lower himself to work with witches?"

"Some witches are okay," I pointed out. While I understood his hatred, in the long run, he was only hurting himself by holding onto his anger. "Like Harmony."

"She's a half demon," Ben pointed out, as if that somehow changed everything.

I wasn't going to pretend to understand the difference. Magic gave me the heebie-jeebies, regardless of who was doing it.

"A witch saved Ivory's life last night," Cooper said softly. ""I know you don't like them, but if it wasn't for her…"

Ben grunted. "Okay, she's one exception. The one Dagen has working for him, Irina, has done some really shit things. She's as complicit as he is."

I stepped away from Jake's arms to sit beside Ben and lean my head against his bicep. "Yeah, she did and she is."

Like her part in the surgery. And then making a sinkhole under my house. I was still salty about both of those. I would be for a long time. If I found her, she would become part of the foundations for my new house. If she was really lucky, I would kill her before she was encased in concrete.

That thought cheered me up a bit.

"It would probably be a good idea to have a witch or two on our side," I said slowly. "If only to stop the ones who work for Dagen from doing anything to us."

Ben's body stiffened. "You're right, we should," he

said reluctantly. "I know a couple who don't have a high opinion of black wolves in general. Or white ones, but they'll help if I ask them to."

It wasn't lost on me how big an offer he was making. If this was a step towards his healing, then that was even better.

"Yes, please do ask," I said. "Thank you."

I remembered his words when I was lying by the side of the road in the rain. 'I love her more than I hate them.' That was what all of this was about.

I didn't know what I did to deserve any of these guys, but I wasn't going to throw their love back in their faces anymore. And I wasn't going to take them for granted ever again. These four guys were the best people I knew and I was a better person for knowing them. A much better version of myself.

"I would do anything for you," Ben said softly. "I know I've said that before, and I will say it again, and again, and again until you believe it. There is no one in the world like you and there never will be."

He meant that as a compliment, but it was probably a good thing. Even the best version of myself was still a fucked up killer. On the other hand, I was surrounded by fucked up killers. Maybe they were the best kind of people and not the worst.

"There is no one in the would like you either," I

said. "Like any of you. You're next level amazing and I love all of you."

"We love you too," Jake said.

"Yes we do," Cooper agreed.

"What they said," Hutton said.

"Same with me," Ben said softly.

I smiled at each of them in turn and kissed Ben lightly on the mouth.

"It looks like we're about to get our answer," Jake said.

I looked over as the Quinn brothers got to their feet.

Kian walked over to us. Tyler and Reed followed along behind like they were more than happy to let their brother do the talking. What must it be like to work so closely with siblings? They didn't always get along, but at the end of the day, they had each other's backs. It sounded like both the best and the most infuriating arrangement imaginable.

"We've decided we will help," Kian said. "You look as though you have decided on some sort of plan."

I wondered if they spent all that time conferring, or just waiting for us to get our shit together.

Either way, I nodded.

"Yeah, we've come to a decision. Not everyone

agrees with it, but it's what we are going to do. Your help would be very much appreciated, and useful."

Kian nodded. "What do you need?" He spoke carefully, as though he still hadn't quite decided the extent of his assistance.

"That's easy," I said lightly. "I need you to declare war on us."

7

"ARE YOU SURE ABOUT THIS?" Jake asked. "It seems a bit...extreme. Even for us." The wry expression on his face said it all. That was saying something. We'd done some pretty wild things over the years.

Selling my virginity so I could raise the money I needed to get away from Helen Dagen was only the beginning. I had no idea then, that my dreams of building my parent's empire back up would actually happen, much less on the scale it did.

I also had no idea that along the way, I'd meet four incredible guys, much less give my heart to all of them. Wait, did that mean I actually had a heart after all? I guessed it did. The jury was still out on whether or not I had a soul.

"It's very extreme," I agreed. "But it's necessary.

It'll work." It had to. Plans B and C weren't options, as far as I was concerned. I didn't get where I was without taking risks from time to time. Sometimes all you could do was roll the dice and hope you got the right pips face-up.

"I hope you're right." He clearly didn't like it, but he didn't argue against the idea either.

"I am," I said firmly. "Would I lead you astray?" I cocked my head and gave him a sultry smile.

"Gods, I hope so." His expression melted into a smile. The worry took longer to leave his eyes, but when it did, it was replaced with a heated look that melted my panties. We were clearly on the same page now.

I stepped towards him. "When you put it that way, how could I resist?" I put my hand to the back of his head and brought his mouth down toward mine.

Before he kissed me he said, "The cars will be here to take us to the plane in an hour." Always the practical one.

"Perfect," I said against his mouth. "That's just enough time, if we hurry."

That was bogus, of course. The cars and the plane would wait until we were ready. Still, it was fun to tease.

"An hour?" he echoed. "How fast do you think I am?" He kissed me, then left his lips to linger on my mouth.

I laughed. "Not just you. *All* of you. One at a time."

He pulled away, his eyebrows raised. I could see him thinking that nearly dying must have ramped up my sex drive to overdrive.

So maybe it did. Sue me. Or better yet, fuck me.

He didn't look as though he minded too much.

He glanced at the other guys. "Fifteen minutes each? Challenge accepted." He placed his hands on my waist and pulled me to him. He slanted his mouth over mine and claimed my lips in a kiss that melted my entire body against his.

He caught me up, lifted me and carried me over to the wide bed. For a moment, I thought he might throw me down. At the last moment, he lowered me gently, then lay on top of me with his legs on either side of mine.

The bed dipped as Hutton sat on the side of it. He made no move to interrupt. Instead, he silently stripped off his clothes down to his boxers and watched.

I didn't know which was hotter, him, or him

watching. Either way, my overdrive switched up a gear. I needed to be touched and I needed it now.

After a minute, Cooper stripped down too and sat beside Hutton. Oh yeah, it was definitely getting hotter in here.

Ben hung back a bit, like he felt the need to watch over us all. His pants were stretched almost to breaking point at the front.

Jake slipped his hands up my blouse, pushing it up off my breasts. He teased one of the cups of my bra down and tickled my nipple with the tip of his tongue.

A quiver passed all the way through me. If my pussy wasn't already slick before, it was now. Dripping with molten heat.

Jake pushed himself to kneel beside me and pulled my blouse up over my head and off. He tossed it aside and unhooked my bra to free my breasts.

"I'll never get tired of doing that," he said with a satisfied smile.

"I'll never get tired of watching it," Hutton said. "Or doing this." He placed his hands on the back of Cooper's neck and brought him in for a deep clash of lips and tongues.

Holy shit.

Ben sat down on the other side of us now. I

guessed he could only watch from afar for so long. He took his shirt off, but he only had the front of his pants open. His curved cock was free from his boxers, but he only touched it lightly. For now.

Jake pressed me back gently and tugged my skirt down. He pulled it off my legs and left me in my damp panties.

He straddled my hips and reclaimed my lips. His tongue tasted all of my mouth, even my teeth, before he moved back down to graze his own teeth over my nipples. While he lavished attention on my breasts, he slipped out of his pants and bright blue underpants. His cock was one of the few places where he wasn't tattooed.

Yet.

He grabbed hold of the sides of my panties with both hands. Just when I thought he was going to tear them in two, he slid them down my hips gently instead.

"If I tear too many pairs, you might spank me," he said teasingly.

I smiled. "I might spank you anyway." I mean, if that was what he wanted…

He kissed his way back up to my mouth. "You're so beautiful," he whispered as he eased my legs apart with his knees.

I had no answer but to sigh as he slid the length of his cock into my wet heat. This was something I wouldn't get tired of. Not for as long as I lived. I would never deny this to either of us again.

I half closed my eyes and enjoyed the feeling of Jake filling me, before he started to move slowly, taking pleasure from my body as well as giving it.

Beside me, Cooper and Hutton kissed so deeply I wasn't sure if they'd stopped for a breath in the last few minutes.

Watching them was so fucking hot, I moved my hips in rhythm with them, driving Jake harder as he pounded all the way into the centre of my core. He panted out his nose a couple of times before his breathing turned to grunts from between his slightly parted lips.

"Gods, El, you feel incredible. I could take the whole hour—"

Ben groaned. "Please don't."

His voice was so strained, he pushed me to the edge of orgasm, but not quite over.

Jake, on the other hand, came hard, with long, fierce strokes which pulled all the way out, then slammed back in and ground his balls against my pussy.

He let out a loud cry like a warrior defeating his

prey. A few more gentler thrusts and he sagged, panting beside me.

He was barely out of me before Ben grabbed my hips and rolled me so I straddled him. I smiled down at him before I lowered myself onto his hard, curved length.

He shivered from head to toe as he slid deep into my body. The groan that slipped from his mouth was guttural, animalistic. For a man who was almost always in control of himself, this was when he let go. Nothing mattered right now but the way our bodies joined and how we made each other feel.

I placed my palms on his chest and rode him slowly, rubbing my clit against him. I kept my eyes locked on his face, even when he closed his eyes. His mouth curved up into a smile of pure bliss.

It faded when I rode him faster and harder, becoming a frown of concentration instead.

"Mmmm," he moaned. "Gods, yes, angel."

I smiled and brushed sweaty hair off my forehead. I doubted I looked much like an angel right now, but I'd take the endearment.

He put his hands on my hips and helped me to rise and fall higher and faster. The friction against my clit pushed me all the way into my first orgasm; a shower of multicoloured fireworks and soft moans.

Ben followed a moment later, bucking hard into my wet pussy. His hot cum made me wetter still. For some reason, that made me aroused all over again. I mean, what could be more enticing than having the juices of two guys inside me, and two more to come? Literally.

Ben fell still, panting before he helped me off and onto my back beside Cooper and Hutton.

I looked up at them both as they broke off the kiss.

They glanced at each other.

"If you're about to do rock, paper, scissors..." I growled.

"No," Cooper groaned. "I've already got rock covered."

I grinned. His cock was certainly so erect it looked painful.

He rolled me onto my side facing away from him and bent my leg at the knee. He positioned his cock at my entrance and slammed into me with so much force I cried out.

"Gods, sorry." He put a hand on my hip and for a moment I thought he was going to apologise again and maybe pull out. Instead, he pounded into me as violently as the first stroke.

I watched Ben watching me as I took every single

firm thrust and gave it back with a roll of my hips. On the other side of Ben, Jake propped himself up on his elbow and was also watching, a smile on his face.

I smiled back briefly, then closed my eyes and savoured the exquisite pain of Cooper ramming himself deep into my body.

His breathing was quickly ragged. He was close to coming. He pulled himself out and quickly rolled me over to face him. He hooked my leg over his hips and thrust into me like he hadn't even stopped for a breath. His hazel eyes were half closed and his lips slightly parted. He was always so fucking gorgeous, but even more so right now, lost in a world of love, lust and heat.

All the good things.

"Gods, Ivory." The words slipped out of his mouth, followed by a series of groans that sounded almost like he was in pain. He gritted his teeth and ground out another groan as he came. Every muscle in his body seemed to tense up, except those in his hips which ground him against me harder than ever. Finally he managed to suck in a breath and that triggered a series of pants before he blew out through pursed lips and relaxed.

"I will never, ever get tired of doing that. You are

fucking amazing." He placed a gentle, lingering kiss on my lips, then pulled out of me and rolled aside to make room for Hutton.

"Lucky last," Hutton said with a smile. He pulled me up into a sitting position and sat facing me. He grabbed my legs gently and pulled me so my thighs were resting over his and my feet were on either side of his ass. He positioned his laddered cock at the entrance to my pussy and slid in slowly and gently.

I leaned back on my hands and lifted my hips up a little more to meet him.

This was a much slower way to fuck, but with his Jacob's Ladder massaging the inside of my body, it was no less intense.

I matched his rhythm. My breasts bounced with every buck. I leaned back on one hand and put up my other to hold them in place. At least that was the idea. I ended up teasing my nipple with the tips of my fingers. Between that and his cock, not to mention fucking three other guys before him, I rushed towards an orgasm and over.

Where the first was like multicoloured fireworks, this was like a shower of silver and gold. My back arched further, pushing me onto him even more.

I dropped my head back and moaned loudly, before I said, "Hutton," in a choked, breathless voice.

He responded with, "Babe," and bucked his hips frantically as he came, driving forward, then back onto his hands, then forward again. He was the last to spill his hot cum into me. And the last to sag and slide his cock free.

I flopped back on the mattress, sweating and staring at the ceiling. It was a good thing the cars would wait, because I needed a shower after that.

8

"HAVE I mentioned recently that this is a bad idea?" Jake asked.

"Not in the last hour," I said. Truthfully, I was starting to think the same thing. This whole thing could go really, really bad for me.

"In that case, let me say how reckless this is," he said. "In all the time I've known you, this rates somewhere in the top five craziest things you've ever done."

"What were the other four?" I looked at my reflection in the full length mirror. My crimson coloured blouse complimented my white hair and contrasted with the black skirt that fell to my ankles. Black kitten heels completed the outfit.

"Offering yourself up for auction is right up there," he said. "Taking on the Onyx Ridge pack in the first place. I don't know what else, but I'm sure there's at least two or three more."

"Compared to those, this should be a breeze," I said. I pulled out a stick of lipstick the same shade as my blouse and applied it to my lips.

He stood behind me so I could see and talk to his reflection. He looked more worried than I had ever seen him before. "I'm starting to think I should lock you in your apartment and leave you there until we get that rocket launcher."

I placed the cap back on the lipstick and put it down beside the sink. "You wouldn't do that unless you lock yourself in here with me. Then you would miss all the fun of blowing up Dagen's house."

His reflection smiled. "I don't mind missing all the fun if I get you all to myself." He put his hands on my shoulders and leaned forward so his cheek was pressed against mine.

"I *almost* believe you," I told him. "But we're talking rocket launcher here."

"I would prefer to have you play with my rocket launcher." He grinned.

I groaned at his pun. Personally, I would much rather stay here and ride his cock, but this needed to be done. When this was over, we would have all the time in the world for fucking.

I turned around to face him. "Is everything in place?"

His expression was immediately all business. "Yes. Everyone knows what they are supposed to do and where they are supposed to be. There is one major flaw in this whole plan."

"Only one?" I asked. "That's better than I expected."

The sides of his mouth drew back. "There's probably a shit ton, but there's one in particular I can think of. The last two times you drove yourself somewhere, things didn't go very well."

"Third time's the charm?" I asked lightly. I was torn between growling at him for commenting on my driving skills, and being nervous for the same reason. I couldn't help what happened the first time, when Dagen's goons ambushed Ben and me. It wasn't raining today, but it still wasn't a very good track record.

And, honestly, I couldn't rule out the possibility that someone in my organisation might betray me.

Like everything else I was going to do today, that was a risk I had to take.

"Elodie." He cupped my cheek with his hands and

kissed my forehead. "I love you. Whatever happens today, I want you to know that."

"I love you too," I said softly. "I intend to be back here tonight for dinner. I'm sure you've already worked out something with the chef. Something healthy, no doubt."

"I might have." He looked cagey. I doubted he'd even thought that far ahead. Not today, when the way things might end was so uncertain.

"I'm sure it will be fabulous." Now I was just talking to put off having to leave. "You should get into place."

He sighed. "Only if you're really going to do this. It's not too late to change your mind."

"I'm doing this," I said firmly. Hutton, Cooper and Ben should all be in their places by now. I needed to get going before anyone wondered why they were where they were.

He looked like he had a thousand things he wanted to say, but the only thing that would come was, "Stay safe."

"You too." His role in this was only slightly less risky than mine.

"Always. That's basically my middle name," he said. "It's better than Lyle."

I laughed softly and hooked my arm through his.

Together, we walked to the elevator and headed down to the ground floor of Crimson.

Staff bustled around, blissfully unaware of what their bosses were up to. I saw a couple who had worked at Scarlett, but who took jobs here while the restaurant was being rebuilt. None of them was left without a job. Most of them worked behind the bars, but one or two opted to work in the strip club, once they found out how much extra money they stood to make. They got absolutely no judgement from me. No matter what position they were in—no pun intended—my staff always got looked after.

Confident that everything was running smoothly, I left Jake there and took the elevator down to the basement garage.

Is there anyone on the face of the planet who likes walking around in these places by themselves? Even Ivory, the big bad wolf, who could look after herself most of the time, didn't like being in here alone. It was dimly lit, cold, and every sound echoed. If anyone was going to get the jump on me before we got this operation underway, they would do it here. At least in theory.

My car of choice today was a convertible MG, white of course, like the rest of my vehicles. For no particular reason, it was one I rarely drove. I made a mental note to drive it more often. It was a cute car, suited to zipping around the city.

I checked to make sure the back seat was empty before I opened the driver's side door and slipped inside.

It didn't explode. Bonus.

I slipped the key into the ignition and turned it over.

When it still didn't explode, I backed the car out of the parking space and pressed the button on one of my keyrings to open the garage door to the street.

The street seemed quieter than usual, but that was probably my imagination. Under the circumstances, it wasn't surprising if I jumped at shadows.

"Pull yourself together," I told myself. I couldn't afford any panic attacks, changes of heart, or anything that might fuck this plan up. "And keep it together." I could flip out when this was over, and I was alone, in private.

The drive was a short one. I could have walked, but we agreed on this instead. I pulled into a parking spot as another car pulled out of it. One hour parking should be more than enough. If not, I would pay the fine. It wasn't like I couldn't afford it.

I ignored my racing heart as best I could, and got

out of the car. *See Jake,* I thought, *I can drive from one place to the other without getting into trouble.*

I waited, just in case my thought was premature. No one shot me, nothing exploded and no sinkholes opened up underneath my feet.

So far so good.

I locked the car and walked down the street a block. I passed several people who were heading in the opposite direction. A couple of them glanced at me, but most of them were engrossed in their phones or chatting to each other. None of them met my eyes. None of them looked twice.

I ignored them as well.

I also tried to ignore the sweat that sprung up on my palms as I approached the Lair. I paused long enough to nod at the bouncers who stood to either side of the door.

They both looked surprised and anxious, but neither made any move to stop me.

My chin raised with as much confidence as I could muster, I stepped inside the club.

The place was empty except for Luca Fisher, who sat at the bar smoking a cigarette.

"I'm pretty sure it's illegal to smoke in places like this." I slipped into the stool beside him.

He turned towards me slowly as if he just became

aware of my presence. "I have to say, you have bigger balls than Alistair Dagen."

"Would that be difficult?" I asked.

He shrugged. "I dunno. Haven't seen his. Consider it an educated guess." He tapped the ash of his cigarette into an empty glass, while he took a sip on his drink. It looked like whiskey and ice, but it was probably apple juice. Sometimes we shifters like to pretend we're the cool kids.

"Where is the asshole?" I asked.

Luca took a puff of his cigarette. "Around. Like a cockroach. He'll turn up again sooner or later."

"He knew I was coming?" I asked.

"He suspected it, but he likes to cover all his bases." He finished his drink and walked around the bar for a refill. Just as I suspected, he pulled out of a bottle of apple juice and filled the glass to the brim. "Would you like a drink?"

"No thanks." I trusted Luca more than I trusted Alistair, but he was still a black wolf and an assassin.

"Suit yourself." He put the bottle back in the fridge and slipped back into his stool.

"I'd like to go on the record as saying I didn't hire you to kill me," I said. "At Dagen's country house, when I asked if anyone had ever hired you to kill them, I wasn't in my right mind at the time."

He nodded and lit up another cigarette. "Noted. And now you're wondering if someone else hired me to kill you."

"The thought crossed my mind," I said. "Would you tell me if they had?"

He considered the question for a moment. "I like you, but even us assassins have rules we have to follow. I can tell you this though, if I was, you wouldn't see me coming. So you're safe. For now."

"Good to know." I leaned my elbow on the bar. "I wondered what happened to you after the bush mysteriously caught on fire."

He chuckled. "Very mysterious. Alistair was pissed, to say the least. The whole place burned to the ground."

"Good," I replied. "It's a shame he didn't go up in smoke with it."

"Like I said, he's like a cockroach. He'd probably step right out of the ashes, good as new." Luca sipped his drink.

"You don't like him very much, do you?" I asked. "Have you ever considered hiring yourself to kill him? You could save a lot of people a lot of hassle."

"Who would pay me?" he asked. He actually seemed to consider the idea.

"I would be more than happy to," I said. After a

moment I asked, "What would the rest of the pack think of that?"

He tilted his head back and blew a smoke ring into the air. "This might come as a surprise to you, but I don't really give a shit what the rest of the pack thinks. Like you, I make my own rules and live by those. But I'm not gonna take that job. Want to know why?"

"Of course I do," I said. I hadn't expected him to take me up on my offer, but it would make things much easier. Alistair Dagen could be dead by morning. We could all sleep better then, especially me.

"I won't take it because you don't do things by sneaking around in the dark. That might be Alistair's preferred method, but it's not yours. When you take out Alistair, you'll want it to be in a way that ensures everyone knows who did it. The problem with hiring an assassin is that there is often a question mark over who paid for it. Believe it or not, there are some black wolves who would be happy to see him gone. Some who might be worse than him, so be careful what you wish for."

That was a risk I considered, but also one I had to take. If I cut off the head of the snake and another one popped up, it would take time for them to consolidate their power and repair whatever damage

Dagen and I did to the pack. That would give me time to decide if they were a threat or not. If they were, I would end them. I wasn't going to let another Dagen rise up in his place.

I cocked my head at Luca. "You said *when* I take him out."

He feigned innocence. "Did I? How about that? Like I said, you have bigger balls than he does."

"You never told me how you got out before the house burnt down," I pointed out.

He put out his cigarette in the bottom of the empty glass and lit another. He took a puff and looked chagrined as he blew it out.

"Here's where I'd like to say I sprinted over to my motorcycle, threw myself onto it and wove through smoke and blazing trees. Somewhere in there, I jammed on my helmet, because safety first."

Ironic for a man who was on his third cigarette since I arrived.

"Let me guess, none of that happened," I said.

He sighed dramatically and blew another smoke ring or two. "Naw, I managed to get on board the helicopter before it left. I had to leave my bike behind. It's toast."

"Oops, sorry," I said. "I'll buy you a new one."

Maybe I should feel bad, but I didn't. It was only a motorbike after all.

He waved his hand in dismissal. "Don't worry about it. I've replaced the old girl already. She was just about on her last legs anyway. But if anybody asks, I escaped on her and not on the helicopter like a fucking coward."

"At least you're alive," I said.

"Yeah. That's what matters." He breathed out a long line of smoke. "You know, for a white wolf, you're okay. Under other circumstances, we might even be friends. Or more." He winked at me.

Once, before I was involved with my four guys, I probably would have been interested in pursuing something with him. Just a night or two, nothing more than that. He was an attractive guy, smart and funny.

And a good judge of character since he obviously liked me more than Alistair Dagen.

I mean, it didn't take a genius…

"For a black wolf, you're not so bad either," I said. "There's still plenty of time for us to be friends though. Or at least allies. Do you have family or friends who work for Dagen? How many of those will die if we end up in a full-blown war?" It wouldn't be a war like humans knew them. We would fight tooth and claw, not with tanks and guns. It would still be bloody, but with much less collateral damage inflicted on children or innocent buildings.

"You said you don't care what anyone else thinks," I continued. "So you shouldn't feel too bad about saving their lives by taking sides with the white wolves."

"Most of my family are assholes," Luca said. "Any wolf who dies defending Dagen probably deserves it."

"So you won't die defending him? " I asked.

He barked a laugh. "Fuck no. I'm only here today as a favour and because I'm between jobs right now. Not to defend him. Not to attack you either. I'm just…passing the time."

He cocked his head at me.

Once again, I had the thought that if I wasn't with the guys, I would be interested in him. Most hot-blooded women would be. He had the kind of hair a girl could tangle her fingers in. Right now, he had it tied back in a ponytail. He was no muscular beefcake, but rather an enigmatic, charismatic guy.

"You look like you have something to ask me," I said.

"We know why I am here," he said. "But why are

you here? Most people don't walk right through the front door of the enemy's territory."

"First of all, the Lair is my territory," I said slowly. "Or it will be as soon as Alistair is dealt with. And that leads me to my second point. I decided not to sit by and wait for him to do something. I thought I would come and have a chat with him."

"And by chat you mean…" Luca put out his third cigarette, pulled out another and held it in his hand.

"Just a chat," I said lightly. "I might give him the chance to surrender. There's still time for him to buy a little house in the country somewhere and fuck off out of our way."

"You know the chances of him doing that are none and zero, right?" he asked.

"I know," I admitted. "But it seems like the classy thing to do would at least be to offer. He wanted me to sign my organisation over to him. There is no reason why he can't do that for me. Imagine the power both of them combined would bring."

Luca made a face. "Too much power for one person. Even if that person seems to be not too shit."

I snorted softly. "I think that might be the nicest compliment I've ever received. Not too shit. I wish I could say the same for Alistair." This would be a lot easier if he wasn't a massive asshole. How different things might be if his parents weren't assholes too. My parents might still be alive. Divorced, for certain, but still, alive. Where would I have ended up then? I couldn't shake the feeling I still would have found my way to the guys, but everything else would have been very different.

"Well, if it isn't the Ice Bitch," Alistair Dagen's voice came from the doorway.

9

I TURNED AROUND SLOWLY, as though I wasn't even slightly concerned by his presence. I congratulated myself for not having a panic attack this time. Instead, the moment I saw his face, I wanted to punch him in it. Or better yet, scratch his eyes out as he was raking his gaze up and down my body.

"Alistair. You're looking well. What a shame. I was hoping you would be in a shallow grave by now." I gave him a sarcastic smile.

"I could say the same about you." He stepped further inside, followed by four of his goons. Two I recognised, two I didn't. "Have you come to surrender or suck my cock again? Or both?"

It took everything I had not to react, except to

say, "If you bring that thing anywhere near me, you'll lose it." Even if I had to bite it off.

He crossed his arms over his chest. "I'm surprised to see you back. I thought you'd run away for good."

"I didn't run away," I said smoothly. "I just took a break for a couple of weeks. I work hard, I deserve it. Maybe you should try it sometime. Have a break for a decade or seven." That should just about do it.

His gaze flickered over to Luca and he frowned. He clearly didn't miss the fact we had an amicable chat. Did he expect Luca to kill me when I walked through the door? I didn't mind it one bit if he was disappointed to find me alive. I planned to keep on disappointing him for a long, long time.

He turned back to me and smiled. "Have you been enjoying the presents I've been sending you? I know I have. I think my personal favourite was the sinkhole. Or maybe the footage." He shrugged. "I can't decide. Maybe it's a tie."

Maybe I should grab his tie and strangle him with it.

"My favourite was when my friends burnt your house down," I retorted. "You wouldn't know how that feels because you don't have any friends. Only lackeys."

He laughed. "That's ironic. You've surrounded

yourself by a man you bought," he counted them off on his fingers, "one who bought you, a traitor and an employee. You call them friends?"

"No." I shook my head. "I call them lovers. It's the powerful witches I call friends." Close enough anyway. "You only have witches on your payroll, don't you Alistair? They wouldn't come and help you if you needed it."

"I wouldn't put myself in a position where I needed help," he said smoothly. "Whereas you seem to enjoy playing the damsel in distress role." He stepped closer to me. "Some people like being the victim. Like you. You seemed to quite enjoy being locked away. You and your bodyguard. You both got off on it."

"Keep telling yourself that," I said. "If you'd like to experience it for yourself, I'm sure I could find a nice, enclosed space for you."

"Are you offering to lock yourself in there with me?" He seemed amused by the idea.

I smiled sweetly. "No. But I'd happily lock you in there with Ben. He enjoys killing people. Slowly if preferred. Cooper too. The three of you would have a lot of fun together."

"You accuse me of having lackeys, but you won't kill me yourself?" he asked. "That seems a bit hypocritical, wouldn't you say?"

I gave him a smile that was all the more brutal because I smelled a hint of fear on him. It wasn't immediate, as though he thought I was about to lunge at him. It was more a general fear of death.

"Oh, I am more than happy to kill you myself," I said lightly. I turned my head slightly, while still keeping my eye on him. "Luca, is there a knife behind the bar?" There should be, for the staff to slice lemons to put in people's drinks.

"Yeah but it's a bit blunt," Luca replied. "It'll take a lot of upper body strength to finish him off."

While Alistair looked at him in outrage, I nodded. "His goons would probably step in before I got too far." I eyed them. The two I recognised looked like they wanted to use the blunt knife on me. The other two looked indifferent. They might not help me, but they might not stop me either.

Luca was right though, I couldn't overpower Dagen by myself. Not in person form anyway. Okay, not in wolf form either.

"You still haven't told me why you're here," Dagen snarled. He was clearly losing his patience and his temper with it. "Are you really so stupid that you would walk into my club alone? You're surrounded by six black wolves who could tear you apart in seconds." His anger melted into a dark smile. "Or have some fun with you first."

I rolled my eyes at the ceiling. "Threatening rape, how original. What happened to wanting to break me?"

"That's still on the table," he said coldly. "Maybe I'll start with your sister, Stella."

I managed to keep most of the cold shock that went through my body off my face. But I knew my eyes widened enough for him to see.

He didn't bother to contain his look of triumph. "You thought you could hide her presence from me? You should know better than that by now."

I probably should. "If you know she exists, then you must know she's my half-sister and we're not close. If this is the part where you threaten to hurt her in return for me doing something, then this is also the part where I remind you that you coined the nickname Ice Bitch. I don't give a shit what you do to her."

Most of that was true. We weren't close and probably never would be. If he somehow made her sign over any part of the organisation, I would be pissed. It would be nothing without my signature and Jake's, so it would be mostly meaningless. On the other hand, I objected to the torture, abuse or coercion of any woman, no matter who she was.

"I guess we'll find out," he said smugly.

My phone vibrated in my pocket, just once. That was a signal from Jake that he heard and would act on what Dagen said. He would send somebody, probably a group of them, to find and protect Stella.

"I guess we will," I replied.

Luca cleared his throat. "That's my cue to get out of here. Before blood starts to flow."

Neither of us was willing to take our eyes off each other long enough to acknowledge Luca leaving.

I wasn't sure what it meant though. I didn't think he factored into the number of wolves who would tear me apart if Dagen gave the word, but I also didn't think he would try to protect me. Why should he? He was in a sweet position where he was. Dagen trusted him, more or less, and I had no particular reason to turn my people on him. And it seemed like he followed his own rules most of the time. I wouldn't fuck with that either if I was him.

I leaned back against the bar and crossed my arms. "The reason I'm here is to give you a chance to surrender while you can. I don't see any reason why we can't sit down and talk like civilised adults, do you?" Except that he was not particularly civilised. Nor did he act much like an adult. More like a spoilt child.

"Let me see," he said slowly. "We're equal when it comes to destroying houses. I am one up on you when it comes to destroying businesses, one up on fucking that pretty little, hot mouth of yours, and one up on making you run away from that charity concert. It seems like I'm winning the war to me."

The side of my mouth twitched. "It might look that way on the surface, but if you look underneath that you would find out how fucked you're about to be. Not literally, because the last thing I would want to touch is your mouth. Sorry, second last thing."

The last thing was his cock, of course.

"You talk a good talk for someone who is as outnumbered as you are," he said.

I smiled. "Are you sure about that? You said it yourself, I would be stupid to come in here alone."

"Or arrogant," he said. "I have another one of those shifter dampening collars in my office. I should just snap it around your neck and see how long it takes to break you."

I held up my wrist and let my sleeve drop down far enough to show him the bracelet wrapped around it.

"I'm so sorry, but I came prepared. This will stop any magic, including artefacts like that. Not even a bonding stone is getting past this baby." I couldn't be healed with it on either, but that was a risk I had to take. If I was so badly injured I couldn't take it off myself, he could pull it off me anyway.

He actually looked disappointed. It was glorious, but it didn't last long.

"I can still break you, no matter what form you're in," he said.

I pretended to yawn. "You're repetitive, you know. Have you ever stopped to think about what would happen if we actually joined forces? We could be unstoppable."

"Why would I join forces with you when I've already joined them with the Quinn brothers?" He looked smug. "I'm sure you were upset when you heard about that. The Ironhide pack has been very generous in sending men to help in the fight against you. When I said you were outnumbered, I didn't just mean here, in the Lair. I will give you one last chance to sign over all of Ivory Claw's assets. This could still be a bloodless takeover. If you refuse, then we will put down every white wolf in the state."

"Huh." I pretended to examine my fingernails.

"Kian didn't seem that ambitious when I spoke to him last. His brothers either."

"Kian mentioned that he visited you in your home in Victoria," Dagen said. He looked like he couldn't decide if he was annoyed that Kian wouldn't tell him where that was exactly, or smug again because he apparently knew something he wasn't supposed to.

"Desperate times, desperate measures," I said. "You know how hard it is to get any of the wolf packs in the country to involve themselves in anyone else's problems. The grey wolves and the dingoes keep to themselves. The other white wolves prefer to keep their noses out of the way. The Ironhide pack was our last chance to gain allies against you. At best, I hoped to convince them to stay out of it."

Dagen was very pleased to hear all of that, of course. He took a few steps towards me. "So, you find yourself very much isolated. You know what I think?"

I raised a dark eyebrow at him. "I'm sure you're going to tell me."

And that was what he did. "I think you know you've lost. Maybe you can't bring yourself to admit it, but you know. You don't want to hand everything over to me because that would be an admission of defeat." He stepped closer. "Your pride won't let you face that."

He ran the back of his knuckles over my cheek. "I think you've come here because you want me to force you to give in to me. Because that is the only way you save face."

I stood frozen. The only thing I wanted to do right now was vomit on his shoes. His touch felt like acid on my face, burning and destroying.

He gripped my throat lightly, leaned in and whispered in my ear. "You want me to break you."

I should have grabbed that blunt knife from behind the bar when I had a chance. I could stab him right in his groin with it.

"I want you to die in the cold fires of the seventh hell," I said.

He chuckled. "You first." He tightened his grip on my throat and shoved me back into the bar. His erection dug into the side of my leg. His breathing was already ragged.

"You pretend you don't want this," he said, "but I saw your face in that footage. You came here today because you want more. I'm going to give you exactly what you want. I'm going to tear your pussy to shreds and leave you bruised and bleeding. And after that, you will still beg for more."

That sounded like a roundabout way to say he had no clue how to satisfy a woman.

His phone rang.

At first he ignored it. He held me in place with one hand, while groping at my breast with the other.

It was getting harder to breathe. All I wanted to do was scream.

His phone stopped ringing for a moment, then started again. He swore under his breath and shoved me away.

I staggered back and put a hand to my now tender throat. I should run, but it wasn't time for that yet.

He pulled out his phone and mashed his finger against the screen. He put it to his ear and barked, "What?" He listened and frowned. After a moment his frown turned into a scowl. "What the fuck? I'm on my way."

He turned his furious look on me. "I should kill you and be done with it, but..." He turned to his goons and nodded. "We have to go *now*."

I was going to comment that whatever was going on was obviously not good, but I was trying to hold back a laugh at the look on Dagen's face. I bet one man's cock never got so soft as his did right then.

To me he said, "This isn't over." He stabbed a finger in the air towards me.

Without another word, he turned and stalked out the door.

The moment he was out of sight, I sagged against the bar.

It took me a while to catch my breath and for my heart to stop racing. That could have easily gone horribly wrong. For a few moments there, I was starting to think Jake was right, that this plan was insanity. If the phone hadn't rang when it had, blood would have been spilt. At least some of it would have been mine.

I pulled out my phone and checked the screen as I started towards the door. There was a message from Jake that read, *Trying to find Stella. No luck yet.*

Just as I finished reading that, another one popped up.

This one was from Ben. *Target in sight.*

Following that was a text from Cooper. *Can I kill him now?*

I respond to that with a succinct, *No.*

He replied back a moment later with a pair of crying emojis, then a pair of smiling ones.

The next message that popped up was from Hutton. I opened it and was just about to read when I almost walked right into him.

He put out his hands to stop me, then drew me into a hug. "You definitely have bigger balls than Alistair Dagen. You might have bigger balls than I do."

"I'll settle for having a cast-iron uterus," I said without thinking. I sighed. "Proverbial uterus."

Hutton kissed my forehead. "We should get out of here, just in case he realises what's going on."

"Yeah," I agreed softly. What was going on was probably something I would need therapy for later. Not that any therapist would believe any of this. Certainly not a human one.

"Do you trust me to drive?" I expected him to say no, or laugh, but he nodded instead.

"You haven't held my past against me," he pointed out. "I'm not gonna hold one accident against you."

He stared at me when we stepped out into the sun. He stopped me and looked sideways at my throat. "Did that motherfucker—"

I touched my fingers lightly to my neck. "It's fine. Nothing I couldn't handle."

"Babe." He shook his head. "That's another reason

why I want to rip off this guy's nuts and shove them down his throat. No one should be that rough with a woman. Unless she wants him to." His expression went from anger to wiggling eyebrows in the blink of an eye.

"I didn't want him to," I said. "But you—that sounds like an offer I can't refuse."

"You can totally refuse," he assured me. "But we can have a lot of fun if you don't."

I glanced up and down the street, but there was no sign of Alistair Dagen or his henchmen. They must have taken the bait. If they were lying in wait for us, Ben would have said so.

Assuming he was able to.

I shot off a text message to Ben and waited. When he didn't reply, I frowned at the phone for a moment, then sent a text to Jake.

Again I waited.

Nothing.

I shook my head and sent one to Cooper.

He responded a moment later with a shrug emoji and the words, *I haven't seen either of them.*

I looked up at Hutton with worried eyes. "What the fuck is going on?"

Hutton glanced around, then hurried me towards

the car. "I don't know, but I have a bad feeling about this. We need to get the fuck out of here and regroup."

"Yeah." I let myself be herded, but I shared his bad feeling.

Something was fucking up and badly.

10

WE REACHED the car without seeing more than a couple of apparently oblivious humans.

What must it be like to live in their world? To be completely unaware of magic, shifters, demons and the fact we basically ran and dictated everything that ultimately impacted their lives. They were probably better off not knowing.

I stood beside the car and tapped my fingernails against the window. I couldn't bring myself to get in, not yet. The guys wouldn't leave without me and I didn't want to leave without them. We could wait a few minutes.

I looked around me and smelled the air, but there was no immediate sign of any of them. Just Hutton and me. I managed to stop myself from chewing my lip. I was so anxious right now I would probably draw blood.

"They probably can't respond," Hutton said. "They're supposed to be keeping things quiet on their ends, right?"

I nodded. "You're right, of course." In answering me they might reveal themselves to Dagen. That would definitely defeat the purpose. The reminder didn't do much to ease my tension though.

"Are you okay?" Hutton moved around to stand beside me. He tangled his fingers in my hair and lightly kissed my temple. "It sounds like things got pretty intense in there."

"You could say that," I agreed. I was rattled, I didn't mind admitting that to myself. At the end of the day though whatever happened would have happened. Whatever sacrifice I had to make to secure my legacy for the rest of the white wolves and all the others who worked for Ivory Claw, I would make.

Some days I felt a whole lot fucking older than I really was. Like right now.

I was ready to give up everything to keep Dagen from taking anything from me. My body, my life, whatever it took. That was probably not a choice someone should have to make when they were still in their twenties, but here we were.

"I hope you realise how close I was to walking in there and ripping his throat out," Hutton said. "The only reason I didn't is because I knew you would be pissed at me." He gave me a level look. "Would you have really let it go as far as it almost did?"

I met his gaze. "If I had to. I knew when I made this plan what might happen. We all knew it."

"We didn't like it," he said. "If it was up to me, I wouldn't have let you near him."

"I know you wouldn't," I said. "I wouldn't have wanted any of you near him either. Sometimes in war you have to make the hard calls. What kind of general would I be if I let my troops take risks I wouldn't take myself?"

"An alive one," Hutton said. "One without a throat which is already starting to bruise."

"Bruises fade," I said lightly. "Dagen carrying out his threat of annihilating all of us would have a much more lasting impact. I will always do whatever I have to, to prevent the genocide of my pack. Wouldn't you?"

"That's the only reason I didn't storm inside and rip his head off his neck," Hutton said. "I have done some hard shit in my life, but listening to that was one of the most difficult. Listening and not acting. Imagining what was going on. It was probably worse than my imagination."

"It wasn't that bad," I lied. "Mostly just a bunch of threats and the throat thing. Nothing I couldn't handle." I doubted any amount of washing would get the smell of his hand off the front of my blouse. The memory of his fingers digging into my breast was seared into my mind, but it really could have been worse.

He could have ignored the phone.

I swallowed down my breakfast when it threatened to come back up. I had vomited enough meals because of that man.

"You're a very good liar," Hutton said. "But I can still tell you're not being honest with me. Or yourself. It's okay to not be okay. If that slime ball touched me, I wouldn't be okay. In fact, I'm not okay that he touched you."

I cocked my head at him. "Is this where you say you don't want anything to do with me anymore because I'm tainted by him?"

"Fuck no," he said quickly. "Nothing would make me stop wanting to be with you. Hells, if Jake can't scare me away, then Dagen sure can't. The only one who can do that is you." He gave me a lopsided smile.

"Good to know," I said. I wasn't planning on scaring him away any time soon. Not anymore.

I lightly kissed his mouth, but drew away as a car slowly drove past us. They kept on going and turned at the end of the street, but for some reason I felt even more on edge.

"One of them should have reported back by now," I said. "How long has it been?"

"About ten minutes," Hutton said. "It feels like a lot longer."

"It does," I agreed. It felt like about nineteen years. If they took any longer, I was going to get grey hairs… Oh, right. My hair was white anyway, no one would notice. In that case, I would get wrinkles. Lots of them. Not the laugh line kind either. The type that appeared when you frown too much.

"Maybe we should leave," Hutton said. He looked as anxious as I felt. His eyes kept darting up and down the street. "Sooner or later someone is going to notice us standing here and wonder why."

"It's obvious," I said. I put a hand on his arm. "We're standing here doing this." I slanted my mouth over his and kissed him deeply with my lips and tongue.

He wound his arms around me and kissed me back. He turned us both and pressed my back against the car. One of his hands wandered down my side and cupped my ass.

He pulled back for long enough to say, "If it wasn't broad daylight…"

"Who cares if it is?" I pulled his lips back to mine.

"Just in time to join in," Cooper said.

The sound of his voice made me jump and pull away from Hutton.

"Where the fuck did you spring from, Pup?" Apparently Hutton had taken to using Jake's nickname for Cooper.

"Out of the alley just there." Cooper waved a hand. He glanced around. "Where are Ben and Jake?"

"You still haven't seen them," I said rhetorically. Obviously hadn't, or he wouldn't be asking us.

Cooper shook his head. "Nothing since I texted you. Ben is probably still following Dagen." He looked at me with worry. "Are you okay?"

Oh, wonderful, I had invited a whole new round of being asked that question.

I smiled and tried not to look annoyed. It wasn't as though he did anything wrong. He just loved me, that was all. I was grateful for that. More than he would ever know.

"I'm fine," I assured him.

He tilted his head and looked at my throat, but

didn't say anything. Maybe he assumed the bruises were from Hutton during the ten or eleven minutes we were alone. That would be a fair enough assumption to make. Much better than the truth.

"Are you okay?" I asked him. His job was to stay out of sight and let Ben and Jake know if Dagen walked past. And then meet me back here. He was disappointed to be doing the least risky job of the plan, but I assured him that at some point he would get to kill someone. Even if I had to find someone for him to kill.

He shrugged. "Yeah. He walked by without stopping. He looked pissed." Cooper seemed like he wanted to say something else.

"I know you wanted to jump out and kill him," I said. "But that wasn't the plan." I cupped Cooper's cheek and gave him a quick kiss.

"I know," he said. "I'm supposed to be the assassin. Sneaking around and killing people that way, not jumping out of alleyways and tearing them apart. Except for those cops." He grinned at the memory and I noticed the front of his jeans got tighter. The guy really did get off on killing. He was something else.

Luckily I liked something else. A lot.

I kissed him again, deeper this time. I couldn't

help being turned on by seeing him turned on. But my worry about Jake and Ben overshadowed all of that and I pulled away reluctantly.

"I should see if Luca Fisher would help with your training," I said. When Cooper looked at me questioningly, I added, "He's one of the best assassins around. You have to be the best to be the kind of killer people know by name and on sight. He only sneaks around when he's working. Most assassins don't like their names being publicised, in case someone comes after them. No one with even a drop of sense would go after Luca."

Cooper's eyes widened and I knew he had another source for his hero worship. And another goal.

"I'd like to be like him someday. And like you. With a scary reputation."

He would have to harden a lot to achieve that, but it certainly wasn't out of reach. I would help him to do that in any way I could.

"Then that's exactly what you'll be," I assured him. "I'll introduce you two if I get the chance. *When* I get the chance," I corrected myself. As soon as I dealt with Dagen, I had a feeling I would be seeing Luca around.

"That would be amazing," Cooper said. "You're

the best." He gave me a big, squishy hug. The kind that let me know I was loved and appreciated.

I hugged him back. "You're pretty amazing yourself."

"While this is all very nice, we really should get out of here," Hutton said. "My bad feeling hasn't gone away yet. If anything, it's worse now."

It wasn't until he said that that I realised I had the same feeling. It went beyond worry or even fear. I don't want to use a melodramatic term like impending doom, but that was what it felt like.

"I don't want to leave yet," I said with a shake of my head. "They might need us."

"I'll go and find them," Cooper offered.

I considered his offer seriously, I really did. But in the end I shook my head again. "I think it would be better if we stay together now." I didn't want to let either of them out of my sight, and I suspected they both felt the same way. Not to mention that if something bad happened to Jake and Ben, I might be sending Cooper in to meet the same fate. That would be stupid at best and devastating at worst.

"Okay," Cooper said lightly. He must have also been in two minds about leaving me and Hutton anyway. He never argued with me the way Jake and

Hutton did. Like Ben, he usually just did what I asked him to.

I hoped he realised he had a voice and that I would listen if he had anything to say. There was a fine line between being treated like the boss and being treated like a lover. I was happy to wear the figurative pants in the relationship, but I didn't want complete control all the time. That would start to wear on us both eventually.

"We should at least not stand out in the open," Hutton said. "Let's find an alley or an abandoned building or a place you own or— Somewhere. What-ever. As long as it's a place we can't be easily seen. And attacked."

"Hutton is right," Cooper said tentatively. "Any-thing could happen to you out here."

Anything could happen to him too, but it was sweet of him to think of me first.

"Okay," I agreed. "You're both right. We are vulnerable out here." I couldn't guarantee that Dagen wouldn't walk back past us. I doubted he would fall for another phone call.

We could deal with him and four goons, but he might have picked up another few along the way. That would mean we could end up screwed. I preferred to know exactly what we're up against, and right now, I didn't. That was unnerving at best, and made me slightly cranky. I thought we'd considered everything that might go wrong in this plan, and put contingencies in place.

Okay, I wasn't that naive. There was always room for unexpected fuck ups.

"We don't own anything on this street, believe it or not." I squinted at the buildings which lined the road. As far as I could tell, none were abandoned, but it was difficult to see inside most of them.

"Want me to break a door down?" Hutton asked. He rubbed his hands together like he was ready to do just that.

"Nothing says subtle like breaking down a door," Cooper commented.

Hutton frowned at him. "If I didn't know better, I would think Jake is starting to rub off on you."

Cooper cocked his head adorably at the other guy. "I'm sorry, I didn't mean to sound sarcastic." He gave Hutton a quick kiss on the mouth that almost set my panties on fire.

Damn.

I cleared my throat. "Cooper is right, though, it wouldn't be subtle. Let's try to find a place and hunker down for a while." That was appropriate, considering they were both hunks.

"The alley I was in might be safe enough," Cooper said. "It was smelly enough."

I realised he was right. He must have been closer than I realised the whole time, but I couldn't smell him. In wolf form I probably would, but in person form my senses were not as sharp.

"A nice, dark alleyway." Hutton wiggled his brows at me.

"What?" I asked him. "I was the one who wasn't bothered by fucking out in broad daylight. If Jake and Ben would just text me back…" I glanced at my phone. Still nothing.

"They'll be okay." Cooper slipped his hand into mine. "They're both careful and probably invincible."

I knew they were the first, but I wasn't so sure about the second. I would feel a lot better if they were.

The problem was, none of us were invincible. The upside of that being that neither was Dagen. At least, I hoped he wasn't. I heard rumours once about paranormals who, while not exactly invincible, were long lived and extremely powerful. That same rumour said they were rounded up by the Witch's Council and killed, or taken away somewhere. Apparently they thought they were demigods of some kind. That would explain why the council wanted to get rid of them. Most witches I knew thought they were only half a step below being gods themselves. They wouldn't want anyone else to threaten their existence or egos.

At any rate, I was almost certain Dagen wasn't any kind of demigod. He was just a regular, asshole shifter.

"If anything happened to them we would know, right?" Cooper asked.

"Of course we would," Hutton said quickly.

Yeah, I would know exactly what was happening with Ben if I hadn't had Paxton break our bond. I still couldn't quite bring myself to regret breaking it, but it would have come in useful right about now.

"We would absolutely know," I agreed. There was no way any of my guys could die without me knowing it. There must be rules about things like that, surely? If not, then there should be.

I wrinkled my nose as we stepped into the alley. Cooper wasn't wrong about the stink. If I guessed correctly, something died in here, possibly not recently. Maybe several somethings. While I liked the smell of blood and wasn't bothered by death, the stench of decay was revolting.

"No wonder I didn't know you were here," I said

to Cooper. "I feel like I should apologise for putting you here in the first place."

He shrugged. "It was Jake who put me here. It doesn't bother me too much. I've smelled worse things."

"Like what?" I couldn't think of anything worse than this.

"Reed Quinn's cigars," Cooper said. "Rotting potatoes. Some people's armpits. Not yours, of course," he added quickly.

"Of course," I echoed. I would have been offended if he hadn't clarified his comment. No one wanted to think they were on par with an alley full of decay, especially me.

"This is the least sexy place I've ever been," Hutton remarked. "And that's saying something considering I've been basically in hiding for the last few years. I've seen some pretty shitty places." He sounded so sad I put my arm around him. He rested his head lightly on top of mine.

"Like where?" Cooper asked. Apparently he hadn't picked up on Hutton's vibe.

"I'll tell you about it later," Hutton said. "It's a long, ugly story. I wish I had come back to the pack long before this. If I thought it would go the way it did, I would have."

I squeezed him a little tighter. We all had stories to share, some less pretty than others. When this was all over, hopefully we would have a chance to tell them and to listen. Or at least to be there for each other. Not all stories needed to be told. There were things about me even Jake didn't know, and never would. That went both ways. And that was okay.

"You're here now and that's what matters," I said. "I love you."

"I love you too," Hutton and Cooper both said at the same time.

We all laughed.

"Awww, you love me?" Hutton said to Cooper. He only seemed to be half teasing.

"I—" Cooper swallowed. He looked at me. "I mean…"

"It's okay if you do," I said lightly. "If I can love four guys, then why shouldn't you love each other? Love isn't a cake; once it's cut up into slices, that's it. Love is bigger and more flexible than that. Love is whatever you want it to be."

"That's beautiful," Cooper said softly. "I—"

Whatever he was about to say was interrupted by the sound of my phone ringing.

11

I ALMOST JUMPED out of my skin. I glanced at the guys before I tugged my phone out of my pocket and looked at the screen. I was expecting to see Jake's or Ben's names under the tempered glass screen protector.

Instead, it was Dagen's.

"Fuck." I was tempted to ignore it. I didn't want to hear the sound of his voice or the bullshit that was bound to come out of his mouth. He probably wanted to thank me for turning him on or some shit. Ugh.

On the other hand, talking to him might distract him long enough for Ben and Jake to carry out their part of the plan. If they could get close enough and everything else was in place…

I sighed, accepted the call and put the phone to my ear.

"Alistair. What the fuck do you want?" I asked.

He clicked his tongue. "Elodie, can you not be classy once in a while? Or at least more friendly to a fellow businessperson. You're always so aggressive. It's not attractive in a woman."

"We're not friends," I said coldly. "I have no reason to show you any kindness or respect."

I thought of him more as something I would scrape off the bottom of my shoe. That was appropriate given the stink in the alley. I might have to throw away my shoes after this. That was a depressing thought but I replaced it with a more pleasant one; that the smell of rot and decay would soon come from Dagen's body.

"I certainly don't want to attract you to me." I grimaced in revulsion. His apparent obsession was bad enough.

"I don't want your kindness or respect, bitch," he said. "I much prefer you to fear me. That's a lot more fun, wouldn't you say?"

I rolled my eyes.

Hutton and Cooper gave me questioning looks.

I shook my head and shrugged. "What do you want?" I asked again. "If this is just a nuisance call,

I'm going to block you. I have better things to do than deal with your shit."

"You'd much rather deal with me in person, wouldn't you?" he asked. "The phone is so impersonal. Although I would be happy to send you dick pics. I know that's your favourite part of my body. Especially near your mouth."

I pulled the phone away from my ear and made a gagging face. "Unless you carry around a microscope, then it would be hard to take a photo of that."

"Hard is the word, Elodie," he said. "Don't pretend that isn't the way you like me."

"The only way I would like you is if you were dead," I said dryly.

"So that was your endgame today was it?" he asked. "I have to admit, I should have realised you had some silly little plan you were trying to carry out. That phone call that drew me away just in time. I should have known that wasn't coincidental. But I bought it. Shame on me. I should have ignored it and fucked you instead."

He paused for a moment before he added, "I'm sorry for that. I'm sure you're disappointed to have had our time cut short."

"Absolutely devastated," I said sarcastically. "I'm not sure I'll ever recover from the disappointment."

"Luckily we have plenty of time to recreate that magic," he said. "Where are you?"

I snorted. "As if I'm going to tell you that."

"I know you're not far," he said as though he hadn't heard my answer. "I would have heard your car."

I frowned. My car wasn't that loud. What the hells was he talking about?

"I can almost hear you thinking," he taunted. "No, I'm not talking about the car engine. I'm talking about the explosive my people put under it. If you turn the engine on, you'll see what I mean. Although, if you're going to do that, let's say our goodbyes now."

I glanced at Hutton and made a face. There was a possibility Dagen was bluffing, but if he wasn't, we came close to being blown to smithereens.

"I have an idea," I said lightly. "How about *you* turn the engine on? If you don't explode, then I know I can kick you out of my car and onto your ass. And if you do, well, no loss. Except my car. I'm fond of her."

"I have a better suggestion," he said. "Have your traitor or your boy toy start the car. There's a camera across the street from it, so I can enjoy watching *them* be blown up."

"You have a fucked up idea of entertainment," I remarked. "I'm starting to think Dagen blood is tainted by psychopathy. Both of your parents had it. Your aunt and uncle certainly did. You have it. Putting you down might be a kindness."

"Psychopathy," Dagen echoed. "That's a long and educated word for a woman who made her fortune by spreading her legs."

"I guess I better hang up to give you time to look it up and see what it means," I said. "Or better yet, I'll just tell you. It means you're a fucking psychopath. Or in terms you can understand, a nut job. Should I dumb it down a bit further?"

"No," he replied. "I think we are now at a level you can understand as well. And your boy toy. Oh, wait a minute. He is better educated than you are, isn't he?"

"There are all different kinds of education," I said. "Some of us learn at school, and some of us learn from life. Plenty of people have expensive educations and are still as dumb as fuck. Like you, Alistair. Didn't you go to the most exclusive boys' school in the state? And the best university as well? The things money can buy."

If I recalled correctly, he did a degree in English literature or something like that. Cool, I might make him quote Shakespeare while the guys tortured him. His last hours would be classy and educational. Win-win.

That was probably just as well he studied literature, really. The idea of him as a doctor or some kind of scientist was scary as hells.

"Money bought you," he pointed out. "And your boy toy. Tell me, does he resent being owned?"

I rolled my eyes again. "He's not owned. He is with me because he wants to be. Because I don't have to force myself on anyone."

"If you say so," Dagen said. "You might want to have a talk about that later, just to be sure. I mean, he probably feels at least obligated. Although, you are undeniably a beautiful woman. You certainly have a beautiful, tight mouth. Why would he not want to stay around a slut like you?"

I heard a strangled sound of anger in the background of the call. I frowned. I knew he wouldn't be alone, because he was always in the company of his goons, but that sounded like…

"Someone doesn't agree with you," I said carefully.

"Ahhh, I almost forgot. I have a couple of your friends here with me," he said.

His words chilled me all the way down my spine. My stomach turned to water.

"What are you talking about?" I asked.

"Let me show you," he said.

He hung up the call.

I pulled the phone away from my ear and looked at the screen as the request for a video call popped up.

I glanced at the phone with trepidation, a word which, in spite of Dagen's digs, I actually knew how to spell.

Cooper and Hutton arrayed themselves behind me, so they could see the screen as well.

"What is it?" Cooper asked.

"I don't know." I tapped the screen and Dagen's face appeared in a square in the centre. He looked even more smug than usual, which was saying something. He pretty much wrote the book on smirking. He should have gone into politics.

He illustrated that point by giving me a smirk. "There you are. And your traitor and your boy toy as well. How nice. You know, you should smile more often."

"I smile all the time," I said. "When I have something to smile about." There was nothing about looking at him that made me happy.

"Well, you'll definitely smile about this." He must have flipped the camera on his phone to the back camera. Instead of his face, I saw the side of a building.

He lowered the phone and my heart stopped.

Cooper let out a little choked noise and Hutton sucked in a breath.

Inside the square on my screen were Jake and Ben. Both were on their knees, their hands clasped behind their heads. They wore matching, steely expressions, which gave away little about the way they were feeling. Except for an edge of anger around Jake's eyes. And half a drop of fear in Ben's.

I stared. I couldn't get my head around what I was seeing. Thank the gods they were alive. They seemed to be unhurt, but… My heart raced and my palms started to sweat.

This was definitely *not* part of the plan.

"I'm sure you were wondering where they got to," Dagen said. He turned the camera back to himself. "When I realised you were up to something, it didn't take much thought to realise they were lurking around. It was just as easy to get them on their knees as it was to get you on yours. Maybe they also like sucking cock. Unfortunately for them, neither of them is my type."

"What do you want, Alistair?" I asked. "Do you want me? Fine. I'll swap them for myself. I'll do whatever you want as long as you don't hurt either of them."

Both through the phone and from the guys behind me, I heard mutters of outrage.

"You can't," Cooper whispered.

"Elodie no," Jake said. He sounded frantic. Of course he would. He would give up his life for me. But I would do the same for him. And for Ben.

"Keep him down," Dagen snapped. One of the guys must have tried something.

I heard a grunt of pain and Dagen nodded in satisfaction.

"Who said it's hard to get good help? I haven't had any trouble at all. It might interest you to know that several of the men with me right now work for the Quinn brothers. They sent them up to help me. They've been very useful."

"I'll remember to kill one of them the next time I see them," I said darkly. "Or one of my people can. I'm sure you don't plan to keep me alive for very long if I give myself up to you."

"Only for as long as we're having fun," he agreed. "Or more to the point, as long as I'm having fun. I don't give a fuck about your pleasure."

I would have made a joke about his lack of skills as a lover, but none of this was funny right now.

"Just tell me where to go," I said. "Let them go and I'll meet you there. No tricks. No nothing. Just me. That's what you want isn't it?"

I wouldn't cry or panic. I put on my best ice wolf calm, lifted my chin and stared right into the phone at his repulsive face. The face that would have been handsome if he wasn't such an evil son of fuck.

"It might be," he said smoothly. He looked like the proverbial cat that got the cream. Or the dog that got the juiciest, fattest steak. Or the… Whatever.

What mattered right now was that he let the guys go. They would deal with him later, without me. I had no doubt of that. I didn't even care what Dagen did to me anymore. I would lie there and take it, as long as Jake and Ben were okay. That was all that mattered.

"Maybe I would prefer to have you *and* them," he said.

"The whole organisation will fall apart without me," I lied. "You get me, you win. I'll sign over everything. I'll suck whatever you want me to suck." It was hard not to shudder at that.

Okay, maybe I wasn't all right with him doing

whatever he wanted to me, but I would still make that sacrifice for my guys.

"Babe," Hutton said softly, "we can't let you do this. You know Jake and Ben won't want you to do it either."

"Hutton is right," Cooper said. "Ben told me once that you're more important to him than his life. I know Jake feels the same way. Ivory Claw needs you. *We* need you."

By the time he got to the end of that, he was begging. He sounded like he was about to cry.

Hells, *I* was about to cry. I couldn't. I had to hold it all together.

I lowered the phone and turned to face them, chin raised. "I am still the boss around here. If I decide to sacrifice myself to save my people, then you have no choice but to respect that. What kind of leader would I be if I left them to die?"

"An alive one," Hutton said dryly. "One with an organisation to run and a shit load of other hard choices to make. We all knew what we were getting into. Especially those two guys. Do you think either of them will forgive themselves if they go free and you don't?"

He gave me a harder look than I had ever seen on

his face before. "Do you have the right to make that choice on their behalf?"

"Yes, I do," I said firmly. "I have every right. I have always taken responsibility for the choices I've made, and that will never change. Not ever." Even if I woke up the next day chained to Dagen's bed and bleeding from all my holes. As long as the guys walked away from it, then it would be worth it.

"Isn't that sweet?" Dagen said sarcastically. "How about all three of you come here? There is no reason why we can't all have a good time together."

"Not going to happen," I said.

"What if I take Ivory's place?" Cooper offered. "I'll even sell my garage to you instead of her."

Dagen snorted derisively. "I have no use for that shit hole. I only wanted to buy it to piss Ivory off. I will take you as well as her. It might be fun to see how many toenails I could pull off you before you scream."

Yep, he was mentally healthy. *Not.*

Okay, I admit I would have a good time finding out how many toenails I could pull off Dagen's feet, but I didn't go around threatening people with it. That was totally not the same thing at all. Right?

"Probably one." Cooper scratched the side of his head. "I have a very low pain tolerance."

"What a surprise," Dagen said sarcastically. "You're a pathetic ballsack."

At least he didn't call Cooper a pussy. Those are way stronger than any balls. As insults go, it's not a good one.

"I'm starting to think this guy isn't very nice," Cooper remarked.

"Right?" I agreed. "This is what I've been telling you since we met. And exactly why I need to get Jake and Ben away from him. At best, Dagen will bore them to death by reading some two hundred year old poetry."

"I prefer Gothic horror," Dagen said. "'Quoth the raven, nevermore.'"

"I've met Raven," I said. "I've never heard her say nevermore." Raven was the head of an organisation called Raven's Gate. They took in young, often homeless paranormal people and trained them to use their skills and be productive members of society.

Raven was a title, rather than her name, but who knew what her actual name was? Like me, she preferred to keep that detail a secret. Every so often, she would request a meeting to ask for help with a young shifter whose skills I could make use of. In return, I helped fund her organisation. Without them, there would be any number of shifters, witches and demons running around out of control. Or worse, working for people like Dagen and Zeta.

"It doesn't surprise me that you like horror though," I added. "You seem to enjoy creeping people out."

"I like to keep people on their toes," Dagen agreed. "Which is why I considered your gracious offer of surrender. But I'm not sure I want to accept it." He looked squarely down the phone at me.

"Your bodyguard was supposed to die a couple of months ago. It doesn't seem fair that he cheated that fate." He turned his face away.

I assumed he was looking towards my guys.

"As for you, Jacob Blakesley, you've been a thorn in my side for the better part of a decade. As much as your bitch has been. I call you lapdog, but I know you're just as much behind everything she does as she is."

"Don't call her bitch," Jake growled. "I don't care what you do to me, cunt, but you're not going to lay a hand on her ever again."

If Jake's tone didn't tell me how angry he was, his use of *that* word was. He knew how much I disliked it, especially to describe someone like Alistair Dagen. He didn't deserve to be called a woman's body part, especially something as badass as a pussy. Ballsack was much more accurate.

"How funny," Dagen said. "You actually think you can stop me, don't you? You all do. It's long past time for a wake-up call."

He came back into view and reached for something.

I squinted. It was a gun, handed to him by one of his men.

Holy fuck.

My heart stopped cold. "No. Tell me where to go. I'll come to you. I'll do whatever you want, I swear." I blinked back a haze of tears. Oh gods, this couldn't be happening. "Please."

"You'll do that anyway," Dagen said. He gave me a last smirk and ended the call.

"Wait. *No*." My hand trembled.

Everything was silent for several heartbeats.

Then somewhere out in another street, the sound of a gunshot rang out.

A moment later it was followed by another one.

12

I STOOD FROZEN for what felt like the longest time. It was probably no more than a handful of seconds.

Then I started to crumble.

Hutton grabbed my phone just before it slipped out of my fingers. "Babe."

Whatever, who cared if it fell on the ground and shattered to a thousand pieces? My heart was in at least as many as that right now.

My knees buckled under me. If Cooper hadn't caught me, I would have collapsed onto the filthy pavement.

Instead, he sat and pulled me onto his lap.

Together, we sat in stunned silence.

I couldn't even begin to get my head around it.

This couldn't be happening. I must have imagined it. None of this was real. It couldn't be.

But the sound of gunshots rang in my ears. Until the day I died, I would hear them, one after the other.

Bang.

Bang.

I didn't need the bond to tell me Ben was gone, I would hear it every time I closed my eyes.

And Jake...

I couldn't start to fathom how I could possibly go on without him. He knew the ins and outs of the organisation, probably better than I did. I was the boss but he was the keystone that held the whole thing together. Without him, what was the point of any of this?

What was the point of living?

I gradually became aware Cooper was shaking. No, not shaking, sobbing. He was silent except for the occasional hitch of his breath, but he wasn't holding back his grief.

Hutton crouched against the wall beside us, massaging his forehead with his fingertips. "Fuck," he said softly. "This is some next level fucked up shit."

"Yeah," I whispered. This clearly hit both guys as

hard as it hit me. We all became closer over the last month, even Jake and Hutton. They still bickered like children, but I had sensed a growing respect between the two men.

Maybe because I told them if they didn't get along I would bang their heads together. They were a little nicer to each other after that. If I had done that sooner…

Hells, it wouldn't have changed anything that happened today. Nothing.

I wanted to cry as hard as Cooper was, but all I felt was numb. The tears that trickled down my cheeks when I was talking to Asshole had dried. The salt felt like a crust on my cheeks. Or maybe my face was numb as well. I didn't know. I didn't care. Nothing fucking mattered anymore.

I leaned back against Cooper. He put his arms around me. I closed my eyes. Maybe, just maybe, if I never moved from this spot, then I wouldn't have to accept any of this was real. Surely it was all a nightmare? I would wake up and find myself in a nice, comfortable bed surrounded by my four guys.

"Now can I kill him?" Cooper whispered.

I took a moment to respond, because answering might make all of this real. I didn't want it to be real. It couldn't be. If it was, the hole in my heart would never heal. I would be missing two big parts of myself forever. The jagged edges of that wound would always cut me to my core.

Fuck, I couldn't hide from the truth either. The cold, hard, shitty truth was they were gone. Somewhere is a street close to where we sat, Jake and Ben's bodies were already starting to cool. Their blood was pooling on the ground beside them. And Alastair fucking Dagen was probably laughing his head off. Shitty ballsack should have been strangled at birth.

"Of course you can," I said finally. "You can kill anyone involved in..." I couldn't say it. "Anyone involved."

I should have killed Alistair Dagen while I had the chance. That was the end game of the plan, but not the whole of it. We wanted to destroy the whole snake, not just the head. Just killing him would ultimately have served no purpose. Or so it seemed at the time.

That was a miscalculation I would regret for the rest of my life. It was one I would have to live with. I made the call. I had to own it. I would have to be the one to explain everything to our staff. I would take full responsibility for it and for the consequences of it.

Okay, I would put some of it on to Asshole. After all, I hadn't pulled the trigger.

But I might as well have.

I put a hand over my mouth and forced a few breaths in and out of my nose.

Could I have been more arrogant? I knew he wanted me, but I also knew he wanted Jake dead. And Ben too, if only because he knew what it would do to me. I shouldn't have let either of them get involved in this plan. Or Cooper, or Hutton. He would kill them too, if he got the chance. I should send both of them far away, right now. For their own safety.

"Babe, listen to me," Hutton said softly. "None of this is your fault. No, don't argue with me. I can see it on your face. This is all Dagen's doing. Every single bit of it. Remember what I told you. He likes screwing with people. Right now, he's laughing because we're devastated. Because that's the kind of piss weak prick he is. He's hoping we'll fall apart, so he can step in amongst the ashes and take everything from us."

He put his knuckle under my chin and lifted it so I was looking him in the eyes. "We are *not* going to let him win. Okay?"

I had no words to respond to him. Not right now.

I shook my head and slipped my chin away from his touch.

Right now, I would be happy to jump into my car and start the engine. If what Asshole said was true, and there was a bomb under it, I didn't give a shit. With any luck, I would reach the first hell at the same time as Jake and Ben.

Although, knowing my luck I would go there and they would go to heaven, if there was such a place. I really didn't believe in any of those things, but I had to cling to the hope I would see them again some day.

Right now that felt like the only hope I had left.

Cooper was sitting perfectly still now. He leaned his head forward and rested it on my shoulder.

"Killing isn't so much fun when it's someone you love," he said softly.

It didn't surprise me that he loved Jake and Ben as well. The guy might have the biggest heart of anyone I ever knew. He would be so much better off if he never met me. Some pretty socialite might have bought his virginity. He could be spending his nights at parties instead of in a cold, smelly alley, surrounded by death.

"Death is bullshit when it's someone you love," I agreed. After my parents died and my heart turned stone cold, I thought I would never feel like this again. I didn't want to, it hurt too badly. Yeah, big, bad Ivory was scared to face loss. It was so much worse than any physical pain.

But then, I let myself care about Jake. I kept him at arm's length so I wouldn't have to face the pain of losing him someday. That was naive, of course. There was no way losing him wouldn't rip my heart out, even if we had just stayed friends.

When I admitted to myself how I really felt, I opened myself up to the chance of getting hurt. I let myself fall in love with all of them. Now I had to deal with the pain of losing two of them. It was so much worse than I ever could have imagined. A red hot poker through my heart would hurt less than this.

This… this was beyond any kind of agony I could ever imagine. And it hadn't even started to sink in yet. When it did… I shook my head. I wasn't sure I could face the next few days.

In spite of that, I wouldn't push Hutton and Cooper away again. Not now. I was done with doing that. Just because my heart was broken into a bajillion pieces didn't mean I was going to hide from my feelings anymore. If nothing else, we needed each other to get through this.

I needed them.

"Are you going to growl at me if I ask you if you're okay?" Cooper asked gently.

For a moment I considered doing just that, but then I shook my head. "I won't growl at you, but no. I'm not okay. I don't think I'm going to be okay for a while."

"Me either," Cooper said. "It's all right to not be all right though. Right?"

"Under the circumstances it is, yes," I said.

"Hutton, are you okay?" Cooper asked.

"Not really," Hutton said. "I know I've said this before, but we should get out of here. Regroup or… Whatever." He rose to his feet and offered me his hand.

I took a moment to collect myself, then accepted his hand and a gentle shove from Cooper. I wasn't sure if my knees would hold me, but they did. The moment I was upright, my Ivory persona snapped back into place.

Elodie could sit on the ground and wallow in self-pity, but Ivory had a job to do.

Hutton helped Cooper up as well. The pair hugged, then they both reached out and drew me into their circle.

I put an arm around either of them and leaned in.

"We'll get through this," Hutton said. "We're still a badass team."

"Yes we will," Cooper said. "We're Ivory's badass team. Dagen will regret the day he ever messed with us."

"He'll wish he was never born," Hutton said.

"I certainly wish he never was," I said dryly. That would have made all of this a whole lot easier. Or not, because someone would have taken over the Onyx Ridge pack in his place. We could have ended up with Gus or Helen Dagen in charge instead. Or someone like them. There were plenty of bad puppies in that litter.

"If I could go back in time I would make that happen," Cooper said.

"I would settle for going back an hour and making sure you all stayed back at Crimson," I said. "Even if I had to tie you all down."

"You would have had to," Hutton said. "There was no way any of us were going to let you do this by yourself." In spite of his words, he sounded regretful.

"I know," I admitted. "You're a bunch of stubborn bastards, aren't you?"

Hutton smiled faintly. "That's one of the things you love the most about us."

I tried to smile back, but he was right. I did like

that none of them let me walk all over them, but it got Ben and Jake killed. Stubborn could only get a person so far.

"What are we going to do?" Cooper asked. "You want me to go and see if there is really a bomb in the car?"

I could hardly believe he would suggest such a thing.

"I'm not going to risk losing you too. That's exactly what Asshole wants." Even as I said the words, they sent a chill up and down my spine. If anything happened to Hutton and Cooper, I would be alone.

Vulnerable.

I didn't know what was worse, the fact I had become so dependent on them and their presence, or the idea of how fragile I would become if I lost them too.

Was it better to love and be vulnerable, or close yourself off and be tough? I decided that I didn't want either. I wanted to love and be tough at the same time. The three of us would draw strength from each other.

Together, Dagen wouldn't see us coming. Not this time.

Some day, the gaping hole in my heart left by Jake and Ben might even heal.

Who was I kidding? That would never heal. I doubted there would ever be a day when that wound wasn't raw and bleeding.

I swallowed back tears because Elodie cried. Ivory did *not* cry. Ivory focused and got shit done. No matter how hard it got.

I had to do just that right now.

I lowered my arms from the guys and took my phone back from Hutton.

"Enough feeling sorry for ourselves," I said coolly. "Our plan had a setback—" I gave Cooper a stern glance when he looked like he would argue with my wording. "A *big* setback, but we're not done yet. We have to finish this. Now."

I turned on my phone and opened the screen Jake set up a couple of hours ago. I swallowed down a bitter knot of grief and anger. I could tap into that well of fury soon, but I needed to keep a cool head for the next while.

I pressed a button on my phone.

"This is the beginning of the end, Asshole."

13

Against my better judgement, I stripped and shifted in that dank, stinky alley. The smells, which I almost got used to, hit me even harder when I was in my sensitive wolf form. So much so, I was able to tell the dead animal was a possum. Part of it anyway. Something had snacked on it.

I nudged my neat pile of clothing deeper into the shadows and hoped my mother's watch would stay hidden in the pocket of my skirt. It wouldn't be the end of the world if somebody stole it, but I would be pissed off. It was just a thing, a possession, but it was the last thing I had of my mother now the house was gone. Well, that and her good looks. I got my uncompromising stubbornness from my father. And, apparently a thing for having multiple partners.

With Cooper and Hutton on my tail, I slipped out of the alley. I took a moment to step over to my car and sniff the underside of it. Sure enough, there was something out of place there. Something metallic.

I would have someone deal with that later.

I trotted away and sniffed. The sulphuric smell of gunshots still hung heavily in the air.

I turned my muzzle this way and that, searching for the right direction. When I was sure I found it, I headed off at a swift walk.

Fortunately there is nothing better than the sound of gunfire to clear the streets. There was no one to see three white wolves slinking through the city of Sydney. The sun would set soon, which would give us a slight advantage but the black wolves an even bigger one.

Sometimes I regretted not being a black wolf myself. Or a grey or brown one. Of course, white wolves were the most magnificent, but we also stood out. Unless we were loping through the snow, then it wasn't a good thing.

We kept to the shadows as much as we could, sneaking behind parked cars and stopping in darkened doorways to sniff again.

At one point, I thought I lost the scent of those terrible gunshots. They got weaker and weaker as the minutes passed. I cursed myself for taking so long to reel and grieve. We should have acted immediately. That was another stupid miscalculation I had to own.

Hutton stopped at a narrow side street and whined.

I whipped around so fast I almost hit Cooper in the face with my tail. I trotted back to Hutton and bobbed my head.

He was right. The smell was down this way. Fainter, yes, but discernible.

I wound my way down that side street, stepping carefully. The sulphuric smell wasn't the only one I sensed now. I caught the edge of the smell I knew all too well. Black wolf. Lots of them.

The further I went, the more overpowering the smell was. Gradually it became stronger than the smell of nitroglycerin.

It didn't matter, I knew we were headed in the right direction.

I kept all my senses open, and moved more slowly. With the number of black wolves I could smell, the chance of discovery was greater. We were too close to fuck up now.

I paused with one paw in the air and wondered if I should make Cooper and Hutton leave. They could get away from here while they had the chance.

The problem was, Hutton was right when he said the only way to leave the guys behind was to tie them up. If I tried to make them stay behind, they would probably wait a minute or two and then follow me anyway.

Stubbornness was both a blessing and a curse.

I resumed walking slowly, sniffing the air and listening carefully. Like any city, it smelled of human waste, exhaust fumes and food. The strongest sound was that of cars and trucks roaring past on nearby roads.

I darted behind a car when a bus rattled past.

Someone a couple of blocks away was playing music loudly. A band practicing, if their stopping and starting was an indication. They weren't bad. Another time, I might track them down and ask them to play at one of my clubs.

Those were the only signs of life in this part of Sydney. People must be hiding in their buildings, hoping there wasn't a shooter roaming the area. With any luck, no one bothered to call the police. That wouldn't surprise me. People often assumed somebody else we deal with a problem. If that was the case, then that would help us to stay unseen.

On the whole, the humans around us were totally oblivious.

We drew closer to the black wolves.

My nose twitched. I drew my brows in a frown.

Something was missing. Something big. Significant.

Blood. I couldn't smell it.

Were there so many black wolves they overpowered the smell of Jake and Ben's blood? Or had Dagen removed them that quickly? He probably had a black SUV handy to do the job.

Fucker.

I swallowed at the idea. Part of me would only believe they were dead when I saw them. If he removed and disposed of their bodies, I may never get that chance.

An edge of panic started to rise, but I shoved it down. In my line of work, I couldn't always expect closure. That was a luxury for people who kept out of trouble. And then not always. Life was never that predictable.

Hutton caught up with me and nudged my muzzle.

I didn't need words to understand his meaning. *We are close and I am here.*

I nudged him back. Unless I missed my guess,

Dagen was at a small park at the end of the street. The kind where workers sat to eat their lunch and stare at their phones.

We could approach the park from several different directions, but I kept heading straight forward. I only needed stealth until we actually got into visual range of Asshole.

Then it didn't matter anymore.

I quickened my pace toward the corner and around it. The park was directly across the street.

I froze.

What the hells?

My heart stopped. When it started again, it rose.

Then it sank.

Dagen stood in the centre of the park surrounded by more men in black suits than I ever saw in one place before.

Kneeling beside them, their hands still clasped behind their heads, were Jake and Ben.

Alive.

I let out a sobbing whine of relief. The sight was the single, most beautiful thing I had ever seen in my life. I was so sure they were gone. Of course, I should have realised it was another mind fuck.

Fine, take that fucking point, I don't care. The guys were alive, that was all that mattered.

If I wasn't careful, my relief would be short-lived.

I lifted my head and trotted across the street in full view of all of those men.

Hutton and Cooper followed right behind me.

Jake and Ben watched our movements. They both wore the same expression on their faces.

I didn't need a bond to tell me they wished I'd stayed away. I was safe where I was. Now I stood right on the doorstep of the enemy's camp, as it were.

But this was still my territory, and I wasn't going to let Dagen dictate the terms.

I bobbed my head at them both and hoped I was able to convey my feelings with my dark brown eyes.

Judging by the expressions on their faces, they understood what I was trying to say. I saw the same look in both of theirs. Love.

I turned my attention to Asshole.

"There she is," Dagen said cheerfully. "You took longer than I expected. Did you take some time to cry?"

I stopped on the grass and looked back at him with cold, predatory eyes.

He no longer had a gun in his hand. The smirk hadn't left his face though. He looked more smug than ever.

"You're as predictable as ever, bitch," he said. "Did you really think I would make it that easy for these two?" He waved his hand at Jake and Ben. "I'm not going to say I wasn't tempted. A bullet to the head would rid me of two major problems. But where would the fun be in that? Now here all five of you are. Right where I want you."

He stepped away from his men and rubbed his chin. "Do you know what the funny thing is? You still look like you think you're in charge here. Like you still might win. Look around you."

He raised his hands. "You are more outnumbered than you have ever been. I hold all the cards. And the pack." He seemed to find his own pun hilarious.

I rolled my eyes at him, but he was right. We were very outnumbered. Jake and Ben knelt in the middle of a sea of dark suits. Had they bought out a bridal store? I certainly wasn't the bride, in spite of my white fur.

"I can see you thinking," Dagen continued. "You're hoping to try to find an advantage somehow. Maybe you're hoping to distract us long enough for these two losers to shift and run away. You might be hoping for an army of white wolves to come and rescue you. I assure you, I have people on every access point. If they see a hint of white wolf, I'll know about it. But so far, there is none. Why is that? Did you think five of you were a match for me?"

I stared back at him. I knew very well no one was coming. That wasn't part of the plan. Maybe that was another miscalculation on my part, but I couldn't change it now. My arrogance was definitely getting the better of me today.

"I like this side of you," Dagen said. "No smart ass comments. No insults. Just you listening attentively to me. Just as you should. I like my women well-behaved and meek."

That didn't surprise me at all. He would enjoy the type of women who would do whatever he said whenever he said it. Who would fawn over him and tell him how wonderful he was.

I wouldn't judge any woman for behaving that way, but it certainly wasn't my cup of tea.

"In case you're wondering, those gunshots went into the sky. Before that though, you swore something to me. Something about an unconditional surrender." He raised his eyebrow at me. "I'm sure you realise by now I don't need you to surrender. I have everything I need without it. The lapdog, the bodyguard, the traitor, and the boytoy. And the slut."

I was starting to hate that word more than I hated

the word bitch. Just because I loved four guys and had sex with them all didn't make me any less of a woman. It didn't mean I was dirty, or tainted, or wrong. It meant I had more love to give than I realised.

"If you lay a hand on her—" Jake growled.

Dagen half turned around and chuckled. "What will you do? You aren't in a position to do anything. Speaking of positions." He turned back to me. "You swore to do whatever I wanted. Are you a woman of your word, I wonder. Shift and let's find out. You can prove you will do what you said you would do, right here, in front of all these people."

The motherfucker must have a short memory. I swore I would do whatever he wanted if he let Jake and Ben go. If he wasn't going to do that, then he could fuck himself.

I still stared back at him.

His expression darkened. "Shift," he demanded. "It's not too late for a bullet through one of their brains." He made no move to get another gun from any of his goons. "Shift." He was getting more and more angry.

I stepped closer to him. He took a step back and stopped. I would have won the staring competition, but he was right. I had run all my options through my head and had none left. I lowered my head and exhaled out my snout.

As I lifted my head back up, I shifted.

Dagen smiled. "That's better." He didn't even pretend he wasn't ogling me. His gaze took in my breasts and pussy, lingering on both before he bothered to look back at my face.

"That wasn't so difficult, was it?" he asked.

I tried not to look at the way his pants got tighter. "A gentleman would offer me their jacket. It's cold out here."

"We both know the cold isn't the reason your nipples are hard," he said.

Actually, that was *exactly* the reason. This man was fucking delusional.

I'm not going to lie. Standing there naked in front of at least two dozen men was intimidating. Some of them looked at me with open lust or disgust, depending on how pissed off they were at me in general.

Others looked away, some with respect and others with discomfort. Apparently not everything was rainbows and roses at Onyx Ridge pack HQ.

I caught Jake's eye. He looked pissed off, like he wanted to jump up and rip off Dagen's balls with his bare hands. That was probably exactly what he wanted to do.

I didn't blame him. I didn't want to touch Dagen's balls with my bare *anything,* but he deserved to have them ripped off painfully. Maybe slowly.

I gave Jake a smile and moved my gaze over to Ben.

He looked as cool and calm as ever. Did anything ever ruffle the man? I noticed a tightness around his eyes. There it was. The first sign something actually was able to get to him. Something that was definitely not good.

I gave him a smile too. They knew me well enough to see past my composed expression. They would know how happy I was to see them both alive. No, not happy, ecstatic.

With a whole lot of luck I would be able to growl at them later for giving me such a scare.

And then fuck both of their brains out.

I turned my eyes back towards Dagen. "The only way I'm going to cooperate with you is if you let Jake and Ben go." I surprised myself with how calm I sounded. "Hutton and Cooper have to be a part of that deal as well."

I didn't dare to look away from Dagen for long

enough to see if the guys were still in wolf form or not. I assumed they were.

Dagen laughed. "You don't get to make any deals, bitch. Have you not realised that by now? You must be stupider than I thought you were. Fortunately, I don't give a shit about your brain. It's the rest of you I plan to fuck with." He gave my breasts a long look, one that would be considered inappropriate by most people.

Most *decent* people anyway.

Jake growled. "I swear to the gods, if you touch her, or even one hair on her head, I'm going to shove your head up your ass so far it will come out the other side."

I couldn't help but smile. I had to give Jake bonus points for creativity. He would probably do it too, or at least try.

Dagen snorted. "Is that the best you can do?" To me he said, "Your lapdog's insults are lacking."

I shrugged one shoulder. "I thought it was a pretty good one. But what he lacks in insults he makes up for in *so* many other ways." I forced myself to look in the direction of Dagen's groin. Ick. I felt like I needed a shower after just doing that.

Apparently that prompted Dagen to step closer

to me. Close enough to touch my cheek with his knuckles. Close enough to whisper in my ear.

"How does it feel to know mine is the last cock you will ever have inside you?" he asked. "The last hands that will ever touch you? I hope you got your fill of them, because they will never fill you again. I can promise you that."

I forced myself not to shrink away from his touch, although it made me want to vomit. It went a long way past revulsion. My memory was kind enough to remind me of the way it felt to be on my knees in front of him. How it felt to be held down by three other men. The feel and the taste of him…

I don't know how I managed not to vomit on his shoes. Somehow, I even managed to keep the panic at bay. For now.

I swallowed hard. "Jake, Ben, Hutton, Cooper. It's time for you guys to go. Alistair won't stop you. Will you Alistair?"

Dagen glanced around at Jake and Ben. "Don't move. I will deal with you later." He turned back to me. "You will never stop being an arrogant bitch, will you? Right up until the end. Or do you have some delusion that I will let you walk away from this? That I would let *them* walk away from this?" The smile he gave me was nasty.

It soon faded, replaced by anger. "You have *lost*, bitch," he snarled.

I managed to keep my gaze and tone even. "I swore I would do whatever you want as long as you let them go. That's the deal. Take it or leave it."

I could almost see the wheels in his brain turning. He was almost absolutely certain I was bluffing, but there was a small hint of doubt in the back of his mind. He was clearly running possibilities through his head. He knew he had all his bases covered and it didn't take him long to dismiss his own misgivings.

He smiled slowly. "I have to give you credit for at least trying. If you were the sort of person who gave up easily, then this whole game would have been no fun. You haven't given up the fight. I like that." He leaned in and whispered in my ear again. "I like women who fight. The bruises around your throat right now are particularly charming."

"Fuck off," I told him. Of course, I realised he didn't like his women meek. At least at first. He liked them shattered. And he liked to be the one to shatter them. Fucking coward.

He chuckled. "That's exactly what you're here for, yes."

He stepped back, his eyes on my mouth, and

spoke loud enough for everyone to hear. "Get on your knees."

14

I REGARDED HIM FOR A MOMENT, my back straight. Slowly, I bent my knees as if I actually intended to kneel in front of him.

The triumphant look on his face was sickening, but short lived.

I stood back up, looked around at all the black suits and nodded.

A bit over half of them threw off their suit jackets and shifted. Including the four who arrayed themselves behind Jake and Ben.

I caught a glimpse of a grin on Jake's face before he also shifted. Ben followed half a second behind.

"What the fuck?" Dagen stared at the black wolves around him, his hands outstretched as if that would somehow ward them off.

Several of them stepped towards him and growled.

It took him at least a good half a minute to comprehend what was going on.

"Fucking traitors," he snarled.

I smiled. "Not traitors. Ironhide. The Quinn brothers decided not to side with you after all." I spread my hands. "Surprise."

If I had my phone on me, I would have taken a photo of the expression on his face. It was a mixture of anger and fear. It was fucking gold.

He pulled himself together a moment later. "What are you waiting for?" he asked his men. "Deal with these traitors."

Being the fine, brave person he was, he shifted. He got a leg caught in his suit pants, but he managed to shake it off and literally turned tail and ran.

"Let's get this asshole," I said. I shifted back into my wolf form and found myself surrounded by my guys. All alive and more or less unhurt. I watched past Jake as Dagen's men also shifted and threw themselves at the Ironhide wolves.

They clashed with teeth and claws, and vicious growls.

I hesitated, torn between helping to take down

the rest of the Onyx Ridge pack and wanting to go after Dagen.

Ridding ourselves of as many people loyal to Dagen as possible, was the crux of the plan to begin with. Of course, that included him, but he would be a lot easier to deal with without the rest of them.

The smell of blood and the sound of tearing flesh made it harder to think. My wolf instincts were kicking in hard. I wanted to join in so badly. To rip and tear and claw and bite and kill.

I could tell from the smell of them that the guys were feeling exactly the same way. Especially Cooper. He was barely hanging on to his own self control. If I wasn't there, he probably would have lost it.

Two black wolves right in front of us snapped at each other. They circled slowly around, teeth bared, hackles raised. Each searching for the right moment, or a weakness in the other. They were evenly matched.

To anyone who didn't know better, they might look almost identical as well. To me and the other wolves though, they smelled so different it was easy to tell who was an Onyx Ridge wolf and who was an Ironhide wolf.

The Ironhide wolf took a few steps back like he

was being forced. The Onyx Ridge wolf, apparently sensing that he had the advantage, got cocky and lunged. The Ironhide wolf leapt aside and let the Onyx Ridge wolf land hard. He twisted and lunged, grabbing the Onyx Ridge wolf by the throat. He gave him a bone-snapping shake. Blood flew everywhere.

I couldn't tell if the Onyx Ridge wolf was dead or dying when he was dropped to the ground, but he was done for either way. Not even a witch could have fixed his wounds.

The Ironhide wolf bounded away to find another Onyx Ridge wolf to kill.

Jake butted me in the side of my head, just under my ear. He jerked his muzzle in the direction Dagen went.

It was clear what he wanted to do. Leave the Ironhide wolves to it. If I timed everything right, a contingent of white wolves was due to arrive any minute now anyway.

They could deal with what was left of Dagen's loyal goons. If there were any left by then. I had to give credit to the Quinn brothers men, they were fierce fighters. I had no doubt the women were too, but they had only sent men because Dagen wouldn't have let a woman infiltrate his organisation. The bastard was so convinced the Quinn brothers were on his side, he let their men work side-by-side with his.

Truthfully, until they shifted I wasn't entirely sure that Kian's assurance that he would help was legitimate. He could just have easily been playing me as Dagen.

I hated to think how big the favour Kian asked for in return for this would be. It was going to be huge, but I'd pay it. It would be one hundred percent worth it.

I bobbed my head to Jake and followed him in the direction Dagen disappeared. The scent of him lingered in the air like a bad smell, but it wouldn't last.

Dagen was a coward, but he wasn't stupid. He would find a way to cover his tracks as soon as he could. What would he do then? That was anyone's guess. My only concern was that he had a backup plan of some kind. An escape route, another pack up his sleeve, so to speak. He might have anything and he might have nothing. When he ordered me to kneel, he seemed certain he won. Right there, in front of everyone, he would show them he had beaten me.

At this point I would rule out nothing.

I trotted between Ben and Jake, my head level

with their front legs. Cooper and Hutton trotted right behind us. Honestly, I would have been happy to drag them all aside, shift back into person form and fuck them all silly. If it was anyone but Alistair Dagen we were after, I might have. I was absolutely determined that he wasn't slipping away. Not again. By the end of this, one of us would be dead.

I mean, he would be dead. I had no intention of it being me. Obviously.

Ben paused mid-trot, his muzzle in the air. He swung it this way and that, seeking the scent.

The rest of us stopped as well.

I sniffed the air and frowned. The stink of Dagen lingered, but now there was something else. Something I couldn't put my toe beans on. I looked questioningly at Ben, then at Jake. They both looked as confused as I was.

I nodded my head in the direction we were going before we stopped. Should we keep going after Dagen?

Jake hesitated for a while longer, then bobbed his head and continued down the street.

We moved more slowly now, careful. Mindful that it might be a trap. Only because we were being so careful did we first feel the ground shake under us.

Following Jake, we all darted for cover under a truck parked by the side of the road.

I tucked my tail in tight to my back legs and let the guys press themselves in around me.

We fell still as something huge stomped around the corner.

Taller than the truck, the creature looked like something out of a science fiction movie. It had a brown hide like leather and huge, round eyes.

It might be something out of a nightmare, but it was also something out of my memory. Judging by the way Hutton froze beside me, he remembered it too.

The thing that stepped out in front of us in the rain.

The moment I realised that, I understood what the smell was. Magic, and a lot of it.

Dagen did have a backup plan. His witch. She created this monster.

I knew a few things about magically created creatures like this. Firstly, they could be conjured from a tattoo, a picture or a photo.

Secondly, they weren't permanent. They only lasted as long as the witch's power could hold it. That could be anything from a minute or two, to half an hour.

Thirdly, although they were little more than a sophisticated illusion, they could still kill us. And lastly, if we killed the fuck out of Irina, then this monster would disappear as well.

Since killing her was high on my list of things to do, that suited me fine.

The monster stomped closer to us. Since it seemed to know where we were, the witch must be close by.

I stuck my head past the truck's tires and sniffed deeply. The smell of magic was strong, strong enough to almost mask the smell of Dagen and the witch.

Almost.

They weren't far away.

Jake lifted a paw and pointed towards Ben, then Cooper. Then towards the monster, and down the street.

The message was clear. He wanted them to distract the monster and draw it away from me, him and Hutton. He sketched another motion in the air to give his orders as to what they should do next.

Both of them nodded. Side-by-side, Cooper and Ben darted out from under the truck and into the path of the monster. They stood in the middle of the street, taunting it for a while before they turned and bolted away.

The monster paused, clearly waiting for direction from the witch and Dagen.

Finally, it resumed its stomping toward the truck and us.

I cursed mentally. It hadn't taken the bait.

The monster leaned against the side of the truck and shoved. It rocked violently above our heads.

I pressed myself down as low as I could go, but kept myself ready to jump and run.

It shoved again, harder this time. The truck teetered to the side, but didn't fall. Again and again, the monster drove itself against the side of the truck.

Bits and pieces started to fall off it. A side mirror, chunks of the side door. The windows cracked and started to break. Glass rained down on the road beside us. If the monster didn't push the truck over, then it was going to collapse on top of us.

I was starting to think it would have been safer to stay and take on the rest of the Onyx Ridge pack, but the choice was made now. We would deal with this as we had dealt with everything else. Or die trying.

Jake looked directly at me and waved his paw towards the other side of the truck.

I shook my head. I wasn't going to run away and

let him and Hutton stay here to be killed. Frankly, I might never let Jake out of my sight ever again. Or Hutton. Or Ben and Cooper once they were back in my sight.

Jake growled at me, but I stood my ground. I licked his muzzle in apology, but like it or not, I was staying.

Jake waved his paw again, this time to indicate that we should all be ready.

Now this I could agree with.

The monster bashed itself repeatedly against the side of the truck, almost in rhythm like it rocked back and forth. If we didn't know before that it was made of magic, we would know now. If it was alive, it would be in a lot of pain.

I almost felt sorry for it, as irrational as that was. It didn't have a brain, it was just a bunch of magic working to order. It had absolutely no control over its actions. What a shame we couldn't turn it against its maker.

Was that even possible? I didn't know. Honestly, I didn't really care. I already knew more about magic than I wanted to.

The monster stepped away a metre or two, then hurled itself back into the side of the truck. This time, it leaned heavily to the side. It teetered for a moment, balanced on its tyres, before it came crashing down onto the sidewalk.

The three of us bolted before the truck even stopped moving.

We loped to the end of the street and veered around the corner the monster appeared from.

The monster pounded up the road behind us, its footsteps shaking the ground and rattling windows and doors. If no one looked outside, they would assume the city was in the grip of an earthquake. A small one, thankfully, otherwise we might have faced dozens of people coming running out and getting caught up in our shit.

I hoped to find somewhere else to hide until the magic dissipated, but there were no parked cars here, no open doors leading into abandoned buildings and, unfortunately, no army of white wolves to back us up.

Just an open street leading through the city.

We were faster and more agile than the monster, but it kept coming. Eventually, we would tire but it never would. I made a mental note that when we got out of this I would get a couple of witches on the payroll who knew how to make monstrosities like this. A couple of oversized gorillas and a Godzilla or two would come in handy right about now. They could smash the shit out of the monster and then go after Dagen and the witch. All without breaking a sweat.

Hells, at this point I would welcome a dragon or a phoenix or two as well. Just because wolves were clearly superior didn't mean I should rule out working with other shifters or other kinds of paranormal people. Even demons had their uses from time to time. Especially powerful half demons like Harmony.

I kept on Jake's tail as he ducked into a side street, then around the corner into another one. It took me a moment to realise what he was doing, but I followed him around another corner and darted past the street the monster was lumbering down. Without anyone to direct it otherwise, it just kept going.

Interesting. Dagen wasn't close enough to see our change of direction. Where was he then?

We loped back until we got to the wrecked truck, then stopped for a few moments to catch our breath.

We seemed to have lost the monster. For now. The ground still shook, but it was a block or two away. Good, that would keep the witch busy.

Now we just had to find the other monster; Dagen.

I sniffed the air but found no sign of him and only a faint scent of the witch. What would I do if I was a cowardly piece of shit? Well obviously, I would leave her to deal with us and run away. That left us with three choices: go back and help the Ironhide pack with the Onyx Ridge pack, try to find Dagen, or deal with the witch.

I quickly ruled out the first option. They didn't need our help all that much and the other two options were more pressing. Reluctantly, I had to rule out the second option as well. Without his scent, Dagen could be anywhere.

But we knew where the witch was. Her mistake.

I trotted off in that direction and left the guys to follow me.

I knew very well how dangerous this was. It could be the fatal miscalculation that actually turned out to be fatal, but it was something I needed to do. The witch stood by and let Dagen abuse me in the worst possible ways, and then didn't even heal me properly. I don't know what, if any, attachments she had to Alistair Dagen, but she was dangerous.

And I held a grudge.

Her scent gradually became stronger. She was only half a block away. The ground stopped shaking.

The magic that held the monster together must have dissipated.

I caught sight of movement up ahead and crouched behind a couple of rubbish bins.

It was her. Irina. She stood scanning the street carefully, but it was obvious she didn't know where we were. She had that cocky, arrogant bearing witches so often have. The confidence they were so powerful, they were all but invincible.

Anyone but a witch would have left the scene by now, but not her.

That, I decided, would be her fatal miscalculation. I could almost taste her blood on my tongue.

Jake placed a paw on my leg and nuzzled the side of my face with his muzzle.

I got the message loud and clear. Don't let anger get in the way. Don't go in half cocked and take an unnecessary risk.

I nuzzled him back. He was right. I was ready to bounce out from our hiding spot and run right at one of the most powerful paranormals in existence. Sure, I had claws and sharp teeth, but her magic could do any number of horrible things to me. Harmony, I knew, was able to incinerate things with only a moment's notice. I would really prefer that didn't happen to me.

I sketched out a plan with my paw.

Jake and Hutton nodded.

I checked to make sure the witch was still there, then indicated that we should enact our plan.

Hutton darted out first. He stood in plain view of the witch and growled.

She turned to face him, her hands outstretched. What looked like lightning arched out of her fingertips. That would be fucking cool if it wasn't so terrifying.

At the last moment, Hutton threw himself to the side and rolled out of the way.

Simultaneously, Jake darted out of our hiding spot.

Lightning flashed towards him, but only connected with the parked car he pounced behind. It flashed so bright I had to close my eyes for a moment. The smell of burning metal filled the air.

I sniffed back a sneeze and trotted out into the open.

15

——————

FOR THE SECOND time in an hour or two, I stood out in the open, vulnerable. I felt less vulnerable than when I was naked, but that was an illusion.

Surrounded by my guys and those loyal to the Quinn Brothers, I was safer standing naked in front of Dagen than in wolf form in front of a witch. Still, this was much more within my comfort zone.

I raised my hackles and growled at her while I stared her down. In spite of how difficult it was for people to tell us apart on sight, I sensed she knew exactly who I was.

Arrogance warred with fear on her face.

Yeah, you better be scared, I thought. We were about to find out what happened when lightning met an ice storm.

I stalked towards her, growling harder.

Before she could raise her hands, Jake and Hutton slipped back out from behind their respective cars and took a place on either side of her.

Some witches could attack two enemies simultaneously, one with each hand. But not three. Her arrogance hadn't slipped, but she was starting to realise the predicament she was in.

On the very edge of my senses, I recognised Dagen's presence. He was close enough to smell now, but not see.

I knew with absolute certainty he was not going to come out and rescue his pet witch.

Welcome to my world, I thought. *Sucks to be you.* I almost felt sorry for her, because I knew how it felt to be outnumbered and pretty sure you were more or less completely fucked.

If she had made better life choices and not screwed with me, I might have let her go. But no one fucks with me and gets away with it. If nothing else, I had to make an example of her. I wouldn't tolerate witches working against Ivory Claw.

She took a step back as we closed in on her. She was clearly thinking through her options, and hoping like hells help was coming.

I matched her step back with a step forward. Then a handful more.

I was within a metre or two of lunging at her when a large white shape streaked towards her from behind.

Ben leapt at her, knocking her to the ground before his powerful jaws snapped around her throat.

The witch let out a pitiful cry before he tore into her neck.

Not loud enough to cry wolf.

Cooper was half a second behind Ben in bounding on the witch. Between them they tore her apart.

I was only a little bit annoyed they didn't leave any for me. I didn't want to fill up on a snack when the main meal was so close I could taste him.

I cocked my head and watched the guys tear into her. Ben really, *really* didn't like witches, did he? And Cooper, he looked like he was having the time of his life.

I let them indulge their fun for a while longer before I let out a soft bark to indicate that we should keep moving.

Neither hesitated to lift their muzzles and step back into their loose formation behind Jake, Hutton and I.

Honestly, there wasn't much of the witch left anyway. If anyone came along they would find nothing more than a few bones and a smear of blood on the road.

I would send somebody to clean it up when we got the chance.

Before we continued after Dagen, I took a moment to lick blood off Ben's muzzle. Partly to thank him for dealing with the witch and partly to let him know how relieved I was he was alive and safe. And maybe just to get a little taste of her blood. It was delicious.

Ben nuzzled his face against mine, then moved back at a bark from Jake. Right, we had time for this later. We had Dagen to deal with first.

We moved in a tight pack with Jake in the lead, all of our senses as open as possible. The smell of Dagen was faint, but still present. Without the over-powering stink of magic, it was a lot easier to follow.

I absolutely didn't rule out the possibility he had another backup plan. I knew that was uppermost in the minds of all the guys as well. We couldn't lower our guard for a moment. Nor would we.

We moved carefully, following the scent while slinking from one parked car to another.

We crouched down low when a bus rattled past, but it kept on going without stopping or even slowing. If any of the passengers saw us, I have no idea. No one would have believed them anyway.

I mean, a pack of white wolves trotting down the streets of Sydney? Most people wouldn't believe it even if they saw us with their own eyes. That was just as well. If they saw us, we might have to kill them.

The scent grew stronger, then weaker, then stronger again. He must be moving, slinking around, hoping to throw us off the trail.

A couple of times we lost it, but managed to find it again. Once or twice, I caught the smell of something else; some other kind of shifter. A tiger perhaps? Maybe a fox?

Whatever, as long as they had the sense to stay out of our way. Most of them did. Cat shifters and dog shifters tended to get along better than the other animal varieties. Mostly because no one wanted to start trouble between different breeds and across species. Wolves versus wolves got ugly enough.

Jake stopped and pointed his muzzle to a darkened doorway up ahead.

At first, I thought it was an abandoned building. I quickly realised it was a construction site. No one was working on it today, because it was a Saturday. How fortunate for Dagen.

It was also the perfect place for him to make a stand, especially if he had a backup plan. Lure us into a dark, half-built place and potentially trap us under falling scaffolding, or the gods knew what else.

I followed Jake inside and we stopped to look around.

Ben moved to stand beside us.

I didn't question his presence at my shoulder. He was the most observant person I ever met. If there was a trap here, he would see it before we did.

In the end, none of us needed to see it. The sudden smell of more black wolves was over-powering.

Three of them. No, four. They must have come in through a back entrance.

Still, the smell of Dagen was easily discernible from the others. He wasn't far, possibly tucked into a corner like the cowardly piece of shit he was.

I pictured him cowering and bared my teeth at the idea. It was as close as I could get to a smile right now.

Jake gave me a stern look which was easily inter-preted. He wanted me to hang back and let the guys deal with Dagen.

I snorted in response. *Good luck with that, buddy*. I

hadn't come this far to stay out of it at the last moment.

He sighed and gave me a nudge with his muzzle. I nudged him back. I don't know what I would have done if I was standing here in this moment without him and Ben. Or Hutton and Cooper for that matter. I would have been a lot angrier than I was. That isn't to say I wasn't pissed off, I was. But having them there with me made it all a lot easier and a lot more fun.

This was what pack life was all about. Hashtag wolf reverse harem goals.

What was the point of any of it if you couldn't chase down a baddie once in a while? Okay, there was all the really amazing sex as well. And the love and support of four incredible guys. When I thought about it, I was a lucky girl.

I would be even luckier when Dagen was dead.

I stayed back a little, with my head beside Jake's shoulder. Ben was close beside me on the other side. Hutton was a little in front and Cooper a little behind.

Something scuttled across our path, but only smelled of rat or mouse. The animal kind, not a shifter.

Yes, there are rat and mice shifters. I wasn't sure

if I should feel sorry for them for being a rodent, or envious they could scurry and hide in small spaces. Either way, I wouldn't swap being a wolf for being a vermin of any kind.

The closer we got to Dagen, the stronger the smell of the other four black wolves became. They were closing in on us while we closed in on Asshole.

In the gloom of the enclosed site, it was harder to see much of anything, much less a black wolf. The five of us probably stuck out like sunlight through the clouds. We couldn't help that.

There was also no chance that the other wolves hadn't smelled us coming, so there was no point in hiding anyway.

We walked carefully around stacks of lumber and broken tiles. I stepped on a shard of ceramic and winced as it stabbed into the bottom of my paw pad.

The guys all stopped and immediately turned to make sure I was okay. I lifted up my paw and Cooper stepped closer to lick it quickly. There was no blood, not even punctured skin, but I appreciated the attention. They were adorable to care so much. I bet they'd fuss over me endlessly if I ever got a cold. Fair enough, I'd fuss over them too. They deserved it.

I lowered my paw and nodded that I was all right.

We all walked a little bit more carefully after that.

We approached the corner where Dagen's scent was strongest, and spread out a little. There was no way he was getting past us, not now. We were too close to let him slip through the net.

I took a handful of steps forward and peered into the gloom.

Gotcha.

Dagen was still in wolf form, huddled against the wall. If I didn't know better, I would think the smell around him was his own urine. Oh, right, it probably was.

When he saw us, he scrambled to his feet and raised his hackles. He let out a low growl.

I have to give him credit for not giving up even when he was screwed. I growled back at him. For some reason, it felt good to do that. Maybe because he was outnumbered. Maybe because I knew the next blood I would taste on my tongue would be his.

He stepped back and straightened up.

That was when I became aware the other black wolves caught up to us. They arrayed themselves around behind us.

I glanced over my shoulder as the biggest one let out a deep growl. *My thoughts exactly,* I thought.

I turned back to Dagen. He must have been absolutely convinced there was some chance his allies would still stand by him. Sucks to be him.

Mindful of exactly who I was shifting in front of, I shifted back into person form.

"Shift," I ordered Dagen. "You know you're outnumbered. Five Ivory Claw, the Quinn brothers and their girlfriend. Against you."

I stood with my back to the black wolves, absolutely certain I could trust Kian and his brothers. The way his men had turned on the Onyx Ridge pack was clear evidence of that.

"Shift." I planted my fists on my hips.

Dagen withdrew into himself, so that when he did shift he was sitting with his knees almost to his chin.

"I beg for mercy," he said, his voice small.

I laughed. My voice echoed back at me. "Like you gave me? Why should I give you even a moment of anything other than torture and death?"

"Because I'm asking for it," he said.

Honestly, if the next words out of his mouth was that *I* was asking for what I got from him, I was going to slap him silly. With a brick.

"You gave people mercy when you overthrew my pack the first time," he added. "And we gave you mercy. My parents could have killed all the children, but they didn't."

"Give them all a fucking sainthood," I snarled. "They only did that so they could look good. I only spared who I spared because I'm not an asshole." I gave him a look, challenging him to refute that statement.

He surprised me by agreeing. "No, you're not. That's why I know you're going to let me live." Reluctantly he added, "It's my turn to swear to do whatever you say. I'll sign away all my assets if I have to."

I smiled. "You mean the ones that are all forfeit now?" I took a moment to celebrate the fact the Lair was finally mine. It better be worth it after all the work I put into securing it. I knew just the person to run it…

I stepped towards him.

Even now, surrounded by the enemy, he glanced at my breasts. If they were the last things he ever saw, then he was luckier than he deserved to be.

"Alistair," I said slowly, "you have nothing I want or need except your death."

He swallowed audibly. "Are you sure about that?"

I cocked my head at him. "If you can think of

anything, now would be a good time to bring it up. I have a pack of very hungry wolves with me and I don't know how much longer I can keep them contained. Except for Ben and Cooper. They had a good snack on your witch. You probably smelled her blood from here."

Judging from the way he shifted from foot to foot and looked increasingly anxious, he had. He must have felt his last chance wither away.

That begged the question. "Why didn't you run when you knew she was dead?"

He shrugged one shoulder. "Where could I go so you wouldn't find me?"

"That's true," I conceded.

"Besides, as soon as my men dispatch the traitors, they will come for me." He seemed sure of that.

"I don't see them." Jake shifted too. He stood with his arms crossed over his muscular chest. Gods, the man was hot, especially when he had that whole alpha male, winner winner, chicken dinner, look going on. Not smug, just confident and comfortable.

Only now I had a craving for chicken.

I glanced down towards Ben. "Can you smell any more black wolves coming?"

He made a show of sniffing the air, then shook his head.

I turned back to Dagen and shrugged. "You seem

pretty fucked to me. As a matter of fact, I think your whole pack is fucked. Even if they're not, they're not going to get here in time. Let me guess, you hoped we would let you stay alive long enough for them to save the day?"

"Isn't that what you would do?" He narrowed his eyes at me. "You would even go so far as offering me your body as a distraction. At least I have more dignity than that."

I eyed him with the utmost scepticism and clicked my tongue. "Alistair, Alistair. You wouldn't offer me your cock if it would save your life?"

Jake made a funny sound in the back of his throat and looked sideways in the direction of Dagen's groin. "Would you want it?"

I smiled at him. "Fuck no. Why would I want what he has, when I can get all of that?" I nodded towards Jake's dick, which was considerably more substantial than Dagen's.

"And all of that." I jerked my head towards the other three guys.

"The point is, I'm certain there's nothing you wouldn't do to convince me to spare your life." I jerked an eyebrow speculatively at Dagen. His suggestion that he still had something I wanted had me curious, but little more than that.

Dagen's tongue darted over his lips. I could almost hear him thinking. He was desperate enough to offer anything to save his own ass. If his mother was still alive, he would probably offer her.

He lifted his chin. "When the doctor did the procedure on you, he extracted an egg. Several in fact. Stimulated by Irina, the witch you just killed. On my orders, they were frozen. They were removed before the fire just in case of a scenario just like this. I can tell you where they are. If you kill me, you'll never know." He shrugged.

His words knocked the breath right out of me.

"You're bluffing," I whispered.

He pulled himself up a little taller. "Not at all. Of course, you can't carry them yourself, but with a surrogate you could have several children. Maybe one for each of your so-called lovers."

Jake was staring at me.

For the longest time, I had no idea how to respond. If I bought what he was selling, then I ran the risk of him escaping at a later time. The remains of his pack might come for him. Or another pet witch.

But if I didn't, I lost what might be my last chance to have my own, biological children. Not just that, I would take away the guys' chance at fathering children. There might come a day when they decided that was what they wanted and they would end things with me.

Okay, I couldn't imagine it, but that might be because I didn't want to. I didn't want to think something like that could drive us apart.

"El?" Jake said softly. I wasn't sure if he was begging me to ignore Dagen or asking me to at least keep him alive for much longer.

. I licked my lips. There was a very good chance Dagen was lying anyway, so all of this speculation might be a waste of time.

"What proof do you have that you're telling the truth?" I asked.

"None," he admitted. "You'll have to believe me. Or not." There was more than a little hint of desperation in his eyes.

It probably matched mine. He wanted to live and I wanted to know for sure whether or not I could ever be a mother.

I looked down at the ground.

At the end of the day this was about more than just me. This was about all the children who wouldn't grow up under the shadow of the Onyx Ridge pack because of me. This was about continuing to keep them safe. The existing children had to matter more than children I may or may not ever have.

Besides, I could always adopt.

"Kill him," I said softly.

Jake and I both shifted back at the same time and leapt toward Dagen. The rest of my guys, and the Quinn brothers and Blair, all joined us.

Later, I wouldn't remember who delivered the killing blow or whether it was Dagen's arm or leg I chewed on. It didn't matter.

What mattered was that he was gone and we were united.

16

I LEANED back in my chair and swallowed down a mouthful of apple juice. Who needed alcohol when I had the rush of vanquishing my enemies? I couldn't compare it to getting drunk, but I was pretty sure it was a lot better.

"This place is going to take some work." Jake looked around at the inside of the Lair and grimaced. "And a shit ton of money."

I shrugged one shoulder. I was too relaxed to bother to shrug the other one. "We have plenty of time. And plenty of money." Once Dagen was dead, there was nothing to stop us from funnelling the rest of his money out of his account and into much better places.

"You can't spend all of it on this," he reminded

me. He glanced at the smartwatch on his wrist. "The next group is due here in about—"

He stopped talking when Cooper showed the latest group through the doors.

"This is Gunter and Carol Frankston," Cooper said. "And the children." All six of them. "I told them to leave their staff outside."

I nodded my thanks and turned to the newcomers. They both looked nervous. Anxious.

Hells, I'd be anxious too if I was a black wolf in Sydney today.

Unless my last name was Quinn, or I was dating four of them. Or if I worked for the five of them. They would get nothing today but my undying gratitude.

I turned my attention to Carol Frankston. Judging by the way her husband was looking at her, she was the one in charge in their family.

"Thank you for coming." I uncrossed my legs and crossed them again the other way. "I understand you have something to say?"

Carol stepped forward, her chin raised.

I gave her credit for having some pride left, and not being afraid to show it.

"My husband and I run the Roam hotel two blocks down from here," she said. "We've never been supporters of Alistair Dagen or any member of the Dagen family." She glanced back at Gunter, who nodded to her.

She turned back to me. "We've always kept peace with Ivory Claw and would like to continue to do so."

I had heard the same message spoken umpteen different ways all morning. Every black wolf wanted to be quick to let me know they had nothing to do with the late, not so great, Alistair. Or any of the people who were loyal to him. I believed some of them. Others were blatantly lying.

They would have been just as happy if I was the one lying dead. Happier maybe, if it advanced them in some way. Those, I would keep an eye on. People like the Frankstons, who had worked in the area for years, and whom I knew on sight, were more or less harmless. They just wanted to get on with their lives and raise their children.

Of course, I couldn't make it that easy on them.

"I know you are," I said coolly. "Did any of you take any action in the past to stop the Dagen family?"

Carol swallowed visibly. "No, Ivory. We tried to stay out of…any trouble. Dagen wasn't known for being forgiving if anyone spoke out against him. Even if they were black wolves too."

Yeah, I couldn't argue with that. Alistair was a pissy little coward, even as a child. He always liked to get his own way. I mean, me too, but at least I was reasonable about it. Mostly.

I leaned forward. "Did you ever help him in any way?"

She looked even more uncomfortable now. "He stayed at our hotel once or twice. We couldn't really turn him down, considering who he was. He would have had us—"

"Yes," I interrupted. "Yes he would have." Just like I had Jake and Ben kill Silas Wheeler and Jefferson Haigwood, Dagen would have had his people kill anyone who pissed him off. I would be a hypocrite if I held it against her.

"We don't want any trouble," Carol said quickly. "Whatever it takes to avoid that, we will do it."

Gunter looked like he was going to choke on air, but he still nodded. "Yes we will."

"Do you have room for more staff?" I asked. "I have a couple of very good cleaners who need steady employment." And of course, they would report back to me. Wherever possible, I was inserting white wolves into businesses owned by black wolves. If they tried anything, I would hear about it long before it became a problem.

"We can make room, Ivory," Carol said respectfully. "If they come with your endorsement, then they must be very good."

Was that sarcasm or scepticism I heard in her tone?

"Believe it or not, I want us all to succeed." I set aside my empty glass on the table. "There's been more than enough animosity between white wolves and black wolves. It's time for us all to come together and put the past behind us." With me in charge, of course. That was the best way to ensure peace.

"Yes, Ivory," Carol agreed. "I would like my children to grow up without having to worry about getting caught up in a war." She was maybe ten years older than me. Old enough to have seen how ugly things got. Old enough to remember them. And old enough to appreciate the relative calm in the city since I took over.

I nodded and gave her a sincere smile. "That's what I want too." Not for my own children, of course, I sighed. I would be happy if other people's children enjoyed some quiet for the next hundred years or so.

I could only hope to leave a lasting legacy beyond that.

She returned my smile and said, "Thank you," before she backed away and herded her family out the door.

Cooper made sure they got out and came back to stand behind my chair. He put his hands on my shoulders and started to massage them lightly.

"Just when I think you can't get hotter, you do," he said in my ear.

"Oh? I do?" I asked. "How is that?"

"I don't know. I guess I just find this whole boss lady thing a turn on. I mean, I kinda like the fact that you haven't just made us go out and kill every black wolf we could find. Instead, you're making sure they know exactly who is boss and everyone knows what will happen if they step out of line."

"I would have thought you liked the idea of killing them all," I said lightly.

"I've been talking to Luca." His tone spoke of a clear case of hero worship. "He told me it's much more fun killing people if they really deserve it. Those people who left, they're just regular people, y'know? And they have kids. They just want to raise them and work hard and stuff. But then there are people like Dagen, who deserve to have their throats cut in the dark or whatever. Luca said it's much more rewarding."

"It sounds to me like you found your calling in life," I said. "I'm glad. You could have worse mentors than Luca. Just make sure you pay attention to Jake, Ben and Hutton as well. They all have plenty of good things to teach." Each one had a unique set of skills and they all seemed happy to pass them on to Cooper. He would be formidable in another decade or so. Luckily he was on my side.

"I will," Cooper assured me. "And I'll learn from you as well. Lots of things." His hands slipped down to the top of my chest and caressed softly. "Like how to stay classy while dealing with an archenemy."

I laughed at that. "I try."

He leaned in to kiss the side of my face. "You succeed. Every day." He slipped his hands down the front of my blouse, under the silky fabric of my bra. He ghosted his fingertips over my nipples and made me shiver. White hot heat went straight to my core.

"If you keep doing that, the next people through the door are going to get a show." Not that it bothered me, depending on who the next person was. If it was one of the guys, they could join in.

"They might—" Whatever Cooper was going to say was interrupted by Luca strutting through the door, followed by a blonde woman about four years younger than me.

In front of Luca, I might have let Cooper keep doing what he was doing, but I put my hands on his wrists and said, "Stella."

Cooper jerked his hands out so fast I thought he might tumble over backwards. "Um, hey."

Luca chuckled.

Stella looked less than impressed. She glanced around the inside of the Lair. "What a dump." She looked squarely at me. "Did you summon me here for some reason?"

I stood and offered my half-sister a smile. "You weren't summoned here," I corrected. "I *asked* you to come here because I have an offer for you."

She and I had never been close. A lot of that was for her own safety. Okay, a lot was also because I never knew how to deal with her. We shared a father and a last name, but that was all. I barely knew anything about her. Her likes, dislikes, hobbies, pet peeves.

If I knew Dagen was already aware of her existence, I might have tried to remedy that sooner. I assumed we had done a good job in keeping her hidden, but evidently that assertion was wrong.

Now I hoped she would give me a chance to get to know her.

Stella looked at me like she thought I was full of

shit. She jerked her head towards Luca. "That wasn't what he said. He said he was sent to keep me safe until you summoned me."

I raised an eyebrow at Luca.

He shrugged. "I embellished a little. Not the part about keeping her safe." He loudly whispered, "She's outspoken, isn't she?"

"I'm right here," Stella snapped.

"Yeah," I agreed. "She's nothing like me at all." Only a lot. She also inherited our father's stubbornness.

I grabbed Cooper's hand and pulled him forward. "This is my sister Stella. Stella, this is one of my boyfriends, Cooper."

She mouthed, "One of?" Out loud she added, "He's a bit young for you, isn't he?"

"I'm twenty," Cooper said. "Well, almost."

Stella snorted. "What do you want, Elodie?"

I waved my hand around our surroundings. "I need someone to run this place. I know you have experience in running a bar. I thought this might be a challenge you would enjoy."

She frowned at me like she was certain I was up to something, but couldn't figure out what. "This place? Why?"

"Why not?" I asked. "I don't have time and I

thought you might like the challenge. I can give you all the money you need to fix it up. You can do what you want with it."

Her eyes narrowed further. "Can I change the name?"

"Of course," I agreed. I wasn't particularly attached to the name the Lair anyway. "You can call it whatever you want."

"Even if it's nothing red?" She looked at me sideways.

"You can call it something green for all I care," I said lightly. "Or pink. If you want to call it Fandango, then go ahead. I just want someone I can trust in charge of the place."

"You can't trust your boyfriend?" she asked.

I glanced at Cooper and gave him a soft smile. "He has other duties to keep him busy. A new career he's training for."

He gave me a loving smile in return.

"And he's supposed to be outside making sure riffraff doesn't walk in," Jake said, as he walked through the door.

"Too late," Hutton said as he followed on Jake's heels. "We're already here." He snaked an arm around my waist and kissed my mouth.

"Want me to throw them out?" Ben asked. He

stepped to the other side of me and kissed me after Hutton and I came up for air.

Apparently feeling left out, Jake snuck in and did the same.

Stella's eyes were wide. She'd met Jake and Ben on previous occasions, when we needed to keep her updated with something related to the organisation, but the guys were nothing more than professional then. She clearly didn't miss the fact things had changed significantly.

What she thought of that little surprise, I couldn't tell.

"Who are you throwing out?" Reed Quinn drawled. He too stepped through the doorway, followed by his brothers and Blair.

I smiled sincerely and without reservation. "Not you four, that's for sure. I owe you a really big favour. I hope I can repay it someday." And that it wouldn't cost me too heavily.

"I can think of a few things you could do." Reed gave me a wink and smiled at me until Blair smacked him on the chest. "What?" He grinned.

She rolled her eyes at him.

"You've definitely got your hands full with these guys," I told her.

"With those two anyway," Kian said, giving his

brothers the side eye. "Some of us know how not to be pains in the ass."

Spontaneously, I walked up to him and gave him a hug and a kiss on the cheek. "I owe you the biggest thanks. You could easily have said no and walked away, but you didn't."

To my surprise, he hugged me back. "I didn't want to have to deal with Dagen on my northern border in a year or two. I know I won't have that problem with you."

"I give you an ironclad guarantee that you will never have that problem with me," I assured him. "And I know I have your guarantee I won't have problems on my south border."

He nodded and stepped back. "Ironclad or Iron-hide. Either way, you won't have any trouble from us."

"We can't guarantee Reed won't stick his cock in where it's not supposed to," Tyler said.

"Fuck off," Reed told him cheerfully. "I'm tame now. The only one who gets my cock is Blair. Now and forever." He gave her a smile which mirrored the ones my guys gave me. Who knew Reed Quinn could actually fall in love? It was almost as unlikely as me falling in love.

Kian shook his head at his brothers. "Anyway. We

just came to say goodbye and that we only lost five men yesterday. The Dagen clan is down by a couple of hundred. If they ever rebuild, it's going to take them a long time. Hopefully not in our lifetime."

"Hopefully not," I agreed. "Thank you again." I watched them walk out the door and turned back to Stella. "Will you at least think about taking on this place?"

"I have no interest in becoming a part of Ivory Claw," she said coolly.

"I'm not asking you to," I said. "Just run this place. You can be the owner if you'd prefer." That earned me a look of surprise from all of my guys, especially Jake. He knew how long I'd been trying to buy the Lair, only to now give it up? If it went any way towards building a relationship with my sister, then I would let her have it in a heartbeat.

"I'll think about it," she said finally. "But if I say no, I want you to accept that. You might own everything else around here, but you don't own me."

"I didn't think for a second I owned you," I told her firmly. "I certainly don't want to. I want us to have the chance to get to know each other. And let's face it, this place could really use a facelift."

"That's for fucking sure," she muttered.

"If you're done," Jake said carefully. "We have a

surprise for Elodie. Over at Crimson." He jerked his head towards the doorway.

"Go ahead," Stella said. "I might take a look around for a while and see if I like the place or not."

"Of course." Jake slid his hand into one of mine and Ben took the other. I gave them a smile, one after the other. How did I get so lucky?

"I'll stick around for a bit too," Luca said. "Make sure nothing happens to Stella."

I gave him a speculative glance. I had a funny feeling he was interested in more than her safety. I wasn't sure how I thought about that. At the end of the day, she was a white wolf and he was a black wolf. Well, no doubt they would work it out between themselves.

"Okay," I said finally. "I'll see you both later." As we headed towards the door, I looked around my guys and asked, "So what is this surprise?"

17

When I stepped through the doors into the apartment, it was like stepping into a wonderland. Every spare surface was covered with candles. Some sat on top of tall candlesticks and others floated in bowls of water.

Scattered here and there were bunches of lavender and scented roses. Not enough to be overpowering, but enough to make the place smell divine.

"What is all this for?" I asked.

"Because you are a goddess," Jake said. "You are *our* goddess. You deserve to be spoilt once in a while."

"You don't think I'm spoilt enough?" I asked

lightly. "I have the four of you and all of this." I waved towards the large window.

The sun had set and the city lights glittered across the harbour like a crown.

"There is no such thing as spoiling you too much, babe," Hutton said. "We decided we would devote the rest of our lives to reminding you of that. Every day. And if we miss a day, you get to kick our asses."

I laughed. "That sounds like a lot of work."

"You're worth it," Ben said softly. I hadn't had much chance to talk to him since we killed Dagen, but he looked like the weight of the world was off his shoulders for once.

"I think *you're* worth it," I told him. "All of you." I frowned for a moment. "Wait a minute, is this where you say you get to kick my ass if I don't tell you every day?" I grinned to show I was joking.

"Just being around you is enough of a reminder," Cooper said firmly.

"And having you around," Jake started. "For a while there, I didn't think we'd have that." His eyes were actually glassy with emotion.

"I thought the same about you," I said softly. "I could have lost all of you yesterday. For a while there —" My voice caught in the back of my throat.

Cooper put his arms around me and gently pulled my face to his shoulder. He rubbed his hands up and down my back slowly, soothingly. If anyone could see him now, they would never think he liked to kill people. With me, he was always gentle and loving.

"When he got out that gun, I thought we were fucked," Jake admitted. "If he didn't like playing games so much, we would be." After a moment he added, "I would be. The Quinn brothers' men would have stopped him before he killed Ben."

"Maybe," Ben said softly. "It doesn't matter now."

"Of course it doesn't matter, you would have survived," Jake said teasingly.

Ben flipped him off.

Jake grinned and patted him on the shoulder. "Love you too, bro."

Ben raised an eyebrow at him. "Yeah, love you, bro."

Isn't bro love sweet?

"Well, we're all here, thank the gods," I said. "In spite of it all, the five of us managed to survive. More or less intact."

"We have another surprise for you," Hutton said. "Actually, two surprises. One big, one *really* big."

"Which one do you want first?" Jake asked.

"I don't want to have to choose," I said. "That would be like choosing between you guys."

"We would never ask you to do that," Jake said. "I mean, everyone knows I'm your favourite already." He grinned.

"I don't have a favourite," I said firmly. "I will kick your ass is just as hard if you piss me off. Now, will someone please show me what you guys are up to?"

Silence fell for a moment.

Hutton broke it, speaking gently. "The big thing is actually at the IVF clinic," he said. "When I was going through Dagen's shit, I found a record of where they took your eggs."

"It's totally up to you if you ever decide to use them," Jake said softly. "We all agreed not to pressure you."

All of the guys murmured their agreement.

I took a moment to process that. So Dagen wasn't completely full of shit. Just mostly.

"Thank you," I said finally.

I honestly had no idea how I felt, or whether I would ever use them. It was good to know they were there if I wanted to. It felt like another victory over Dagen. Something he tried to take, but in the end he didn't. My only regret was that I didn't ask him why he bothered to keep the eggs in the first place. It was probably some kind of mind game he wanted to play. Now he would never be able to.

"What's the other surprise?" I asked. I was already feeling somewhat overwhelmed at this point anyway.

Overwhelmed in a good way. I couldn't ask for much more than they already gave me.

"It's in the bedroom," Ben said.

Okay, I should have seen that coming. Four horny guys wanted to give me something in the bedroom.

What a shock.

"It's not what you think," Cooper said quickly. He knitted his brows. "Well it is, but it isn't."

"Didn't you say you went to university?" Jake teased.

Cooper flipped him off.

Jake pretended to huff. "Remember when they respected me?"

"Nope." Hutton grinned.

Now it was Jake's turn to give him the finger. "Fuck off, bro."

I raised my eyebrows at him. That was a big step up from 'traitor.' Frankly, all this bro love was turning me on.

I grabbed Ben's hand. "So, what did you want to show me in the bedroom?"

He smiled and walked beside me.

We stopped in the doorway.

I gaped. "Holy shit."

My bed was gone, replaced by one wide enough for about ten people to sleep.

"Yes! Now I have room for all those pet cats I was going to get." I grinned.

"As long as they're tigers shifters and aren't assholes," Jake said. "Lions would be okay too."

"You don't think four guys is enough?" I asked.

"I think," Jake said slowly, "that we love you and want you to be happy. Whatever it takes to make that happen, we're okay with it."

"We also put some smaller beds in the other bedrooms in case you want to be alone," Ben said.

"I do like to spread out sometimes," I said. Maybe not *this* much though. All five of us could share the bed and not touch each other. "I'd like to see how comfortable it is. Who wants to join me?"

Predictably, we all kicked off our shoes and lay down together.

Ben snagged a spot on one side of me and Jake on the other. Hutton and Cooper both lay on the other side of Ben.

I wriggled down into the mattress. "This is exactly the right combination of not too hard and not too soft." It didn't surprise me at all they nailed that. I was very particular with the mattresses I slept on. After spending ten years on a narrow, almost flat foam one, I swore I would never be uncomfortable like that again. In this department, I was more like a domestic dog than a wild wolf, and I was okay with that.

Life was too fucking short to be uncomfortable.

"That's funny," Jake said. "I am also the perfect combination of not too hard and not too soft."

I rolled over and raised an eyebrow at him. "Where are you soft?" I poked him in the chest with the tip of my fingernail. "You feel like a rock to me."

He smiled. "I'm just a soft puppy dog on the inside. At least where you are concerned."

I smiled back. "That's true." There was nothing he wouldn't give me or do for me if it made me happy.

Same for the other guys. That went both ways. If they needed me to move heaven and earth, then I would do it. At least I could rock their world for a little while.

I scooted over to press my mouth to Jake's. Just lightly at first, then with more tongue and teeth and heat.

Before he could even touch me or catch his breath, I worked my way down his body, caressing through his clothes. I finally stopped at the top of his jeans. I eased the button loose and slid down the zipper before I tugged the front down his thighs. I took pity on his thick erection, by also pulling down the front of his bright green underpants. I even ignored the fact he had small turtles printed on the front of them.

Cute.

And then I found myself face to tip with his cock. My heart started to race and sweat broke out on my palms.

"El, you don't have to do that," he said softly. "I know it's hard... I mean, difficult." It was certainly *hard*. "I understand."

"We all do," Ben said. "None of us will ever ask you to do anything you don't want to do."

That was good, because I was notoriously stubborn. But this...

"I want to," I said, my voice soft but firm. It was something I enjoyed doing and I wasn't going to let anyone take it away from me anymore.

That didn't mean I dove straight in though. I gripped the base of his shaft and started to run the tip of my tongue feather lightly over the side of Jake's cock.

I loved the shiver that passed through him at that slight touch. I missed that. Everything I did with these guys made me feel powerful, like a goddess. But in this, I felt like I was in complete control.

One of the guys moved around behind me, unfastened my skirt and started to slide it down my hips.

I lifted myself up to help them, not even caring that I had no idea which of them it was.

My panties followed. A large hand gently bent my knee and slid in between my thighs to caress my clit.

I circled the tip of Jake's cock, tasting his precum and the salty warmth of his skin. I looked up at him and saw him watching me.

His eyes were filled with a combination of concern, desire and love.

I knew he wanted me to take him deep into my mouth, but not if it was something I would regret.

Since I couldn't imagine a universe in which I would regret sucking any of them off, I did the former. I closed my mouth around as much of his length as I could fit without choking. And then a little more. I ran my tongue up and down him and then started to suck while my hands caressed his balls.

At the same time, whoever was behind me slipped a finger inside me. Then another. And another.

Judging by the feeling of calluses against my skin, it was Hutton. He had the roughest, but at the same time, gentlest hands. He circled my clit with his thumb while he massaged inside my body with his fingertips.

Ben moved down the mattress and started to unbutton my blouse and unhook my bra to let my breasts fall free. I lifted first one arm, then the other so he could pull straps and sleeves out of the way.

He looked me in the eyes and smiled before he started to lick and suck my breasts and nipples. Obviously he remembered from when we still had the bond, that I loved this more than almost anything.

He didn't seem to mind it too much either.

I glanced back up at Jake to see he'd closed his eyes. He didn't look worried anymore. That expression was replaced with one of ecstasy.

I closed my own eyes and let the sensations from Hutton's fingers course through me. I found a rhythm of caresses and sucks and licks that drove me closer and closer before I fell into oblivion. I had to take my mouth off Jake's cock so I could breathe and let out a series of soft moans, while I came. Before I was even back down to earth, I latched back on and sucked harder than ever.

Tender hands pried my legs open a little further, and a warm, pierced cock slid into my body. Definitely Hutton.

"There's lube in the drawer over there," Hutton said.

I wasn't sure who he was speaking to until I heard Cooper say, "Are you sure?"

My eyes widened. Holy shit. Just thinking about Cooper fucking Hutton's ass, while Hutton fucked my pussy almost made me come again.

I looked over to Ben. His eyebrows were raised, but that was the only sign he'd heard. He was obviously not going to judge them any more than I was.

I glanced up at Jake. To my surprise, he'd propped himself up on his elbow and seemed to be watching the other guys.

He must have sensed me looking, because his gaze turned to me and he shrugged one shoulder.

I wondered if he would be into that. That thought made me suck harder.

Jake groaned and rolled his hips, pushing his

cock so deep down my throat I could barely breathe. I took in every millimetre and sucked faster.

Hutton's slow thrusts stopped for a few moments. I pictured Cooper's fingers smearing lube onto his rear hole. When he started to move again, it was more careful, slower. I knew, without looking, that Cooper had slid inside him.

Holy gods.

Apparently Jake agreed with that, because a shudder passed through his whole body and he came, spilling hot cum deep into my mouth.

I swallowed, savouring the taste on my tongue. He really was delicious.

I let his cock go and glanced over my shoulder. Sure enough, Cooper knelt behind Hutton, who was lying behind me. All three of our hips were moving in perfect rhythm.

I turned my face back toward Ben. He hadn't stopped spoiling my breasts since he started.

He stopped now, to look up at me questioningly.

"Can I have your cock in my mouth?" I asked softly.

"Any time," he said. Jake moved over to let him in. He slowly, gently slid his curved cock between my lips.

The taste and feel of him was different to Jake's.

Just as tasty, but with a flavour that was uniquely Ben's.

I barely started sucking him when Hutton gasped and thrust a little harder and faster into my body.

"Oh, gods," he ground out. "Fuck, fuck, fuck. Yeah…" He filled my pussy with his warm cum. He panted, then mercifully pulled Cooper down to the end of the bed where I could see them. And watch. And enjoy the sight of Hutton lying on his stomach while Cooper knelt between his thighs.

Jake moved around behind me and slipped his hand between my wet thighs. He circled my clit with his fingertips, while his other hand traced lines over my bare ass. He had me panting in a matter of moments.

When I came again, I clamped my lips down on Ben's cock, drawing an orgasm out of him too. At the same time, Cooper thrust a couple of more times into Hutton's ass before he joined us in orgasmland.

I swallowed down Ben's creamy juices before I came down from the most intense, wonderful orgasm I ever had.

I lay there for a long while before I slid my mouth off his cock. Jake took his hand away from my pussy and gave a long, contented sigh. Ben and

Jake relaxed on either side of me. Hutton and Cooper lay on the other side of Ben, and cuddled.

Everyone snuggled in closer, like we were a litter of content, milk drunk puppies.

"I love you guys," I whispered.

"I love you too," they said back, more or less in unison.

I sighed with contentment and snuggled down a little deeper. What in the world could be better than being naked in bed with the four hottest, sexiest, smartest, most loving guys in the entire universe?

I couldn't think of a single, fucking thing.

EPILOGUE

STELLA

"You don't have to babysit me, you know," I said to Luca. He seemed to think I had no idea who he was or what he was. Okay, I tried to spend as much time having nothing to do with Ivory Claw as I could, but I knew a killer when I smelled one. And a black wolf. I didn't want anything to do with them either.

I didn't remember my father. My mother said very little about him, but I knew who he was too. Head of the organisation before my sister. Criminal, killer.

From all accounts, the Onyx Ridge pack was worse, but my father was no saint. Neither was my sister.

She and Jake seemed to think I needed to be kept

in the loop about the organisation, given an *education.*

I learnt enough to know an assassin when I met one. Just because he was sexy as fuck didn't mean I was going to get drawn into whatever story he seemed to think I should fit into.

"That's good," he said lightly. "Because babysitting doesn't pay very well. I'm just here out of curiosity."

I placed one fist on my hip. "Yeah? About what?"

"Lots of things," he said as if that answered anything. "This place. You. What is it about you that your sister would just hand the club over to you? Ivory is—how do I put this politely—a control freak."

I snorted. "Her name is Elodie, and tell me about it. She wants to stop me from becoming a target, but at the same time she really wants me to be a part of her shit." And what a lot of shit it was. This club was run down, tired. If it was an animal it would probably be put to sleep. As it was, it should probably be torn down or blown up.

Luca leaned his elbow on the bar. "Question is, are you gonna be a part of it?"

The look he gave me was so hot I should probably have caught on fire. Or my panties anyway. He had that dangerous-as-hells thing going on. The thing I spent the last twenty-two years of my life staying the fuck away from. I wasn't going to change that now just because my pulse hammered through my body.

"I don't know," I admitted.

ABOUT THE AUTHOR

Maggie Alabaster writes reverse harem and, paranormal, sci-fi and fantasy romance.

She lives in NSW, Australia with one spouse, two daughters, one dog, and countless birds.

Sign up for my newsletter! Sign Up!

Join my reader group! Join here!

Follow me on Bookbub! Click here to follow me!

Check out my website- www.maggiealabaster.com

Breakaway

Power Play

Brutal Academy

Book 1 Heartless

Book 2 Cruel

Book 3 Vengeful

Court of Blood and Binding

Book 1 Song of Scent and Magic

Book 2 Crown of Mist and Heat

Book 3 Sword of Balm and Shadow

Book 4 Whisper of Frost and Flame

Dark Masque

Book 1 Bait

Book 2 Prey

Book 3 Trap

Saving Abbie

Book 1 Pitch

Book 2 Pound

Book 3 Session

Book 4 Muse

Book 5 Rhythm

Book 6 Encore

Novella Venomous

Saving Abbie books 1-4

Saving Abbie books 4-6 + Venomous

Ruthless Claws

Book 1 Ivory

Book 2 Crimson

Book 3 Elodie

Harmony's Magic

Book 1 Summoned by Fire

Book 2 Summoned by Fate

Book 3 Summoned by Desire

Shifter's Vault

Book 1 Discarded

Book 2 Deceived

Book 3 Disgraced

My Alien Mates

Book 1 Star Warriors

Book 2 Star Defenders

Book 3 Star Protectors

Academy of Modern Magic

Book 1 Digital Magic

Book 2 Virtual Magic

Book 3 Logical Magic

Complete Collection

Summer's Harem

Book 1: Shimmer

Book 2: Glimmer

Book 3: Flicker

Complete collection

Short reads

Taken by the Snowmen

Jingle All the Way

Also by Maggie Alabaster and Erin Yoshikawa

Caught by the Tide

Book 1–Pursued by Shadows

Book 2 Pursued by Darkness

Book 3 Pursued by Monsters